LEE COUNTY LIBRARY
107 HAWKINS AVE.
SANFORD, N. C. 27330

THE TEN-DAY QUEEN

When he named his cousin Lady Jane Grey as his heir, the boy-king Edward VI left her not a crown but a cross. Remarkably well-educated, Jane was a pawn in the royal game of chess, forever under check to the crown. She married as a child to please her designing parents, and died on the block for their ambitions. One cannot believe that this girl was capable of doing harm, but her death was inevitable. Her story is well known, but it is interesting to wonder what would have happened had she lived.

THE TEN-DAY QUEEN

URSULA BLOOM
as Lozania Prole

A Lythway Book

**CHIVERS PRESS
BATH**

First published in Great Britain 1972
by
Robert Hale & Company
This Large Print edition published by
Chivers Press
by arrangement with the author
1983

ISBN 0 85119 916 X

© Lozania Prole 1972

British Library Cataloguing in Publication Data

Bloom, Ursula
   The ten-day queen.—Large print ed.—(A Lythway book)
   I. Title
823′.912[F]   PR6003.L58

ISBN 0–85119–916–X

To
Lornie Leete-Hodge
with
grateful thanks for her help

Guide to Kingship

King Henry the Eighth	1509–1547
King Edward the Sixth	1547–1553
Queen Jane	1553 for ten days only
Queen Mary Tudor	1553–1558
Queen Elizabeth the First	1558–1603

PREFACE

When Long Tom started to toll for the demise of King Henry the Eighth, on that frosty night in the January of 1547, few realized what a mêlée of one king and three queens would come into line. The world was in a state of confusion.

The Church of England had been installed properly by the boy king, Edward VI, thus fulfilling one of the last promises to his dying father. In this he was backed by his sister, Elizabeth, and his cousin, Jane, but violently opposed by his eldest sister, the Princess Mary, whose rigorous devotion and dedication to the Catholic faith was a bubbling volcano in the land. Too many had died already, and this was not going to be the end of it, for more would go!

One of the most curious points about the dead King, who could, when in the mood, be one of the most diabolical men for vengeance who ever went to the Stone of Scone for crowning, was that he had always had a surprising devotion for children.

He would allow the little Princess Elizabeth to pull his beard and really hurt him. He was an expert in the delights of a piggy-back and even if—as time progressed—he limped slightly when playing hide-and-seek along the draughty passages of Whitehall Palace, and Hampton

Court, he never hesitated to join in the game to amuse the children.

The Princess Mary was never attractive; her mother's own daughter, (and that poor lady had suffered far too much) it might have seemed that the babe had been born with sour grapes in her mouth. She was delicate, a miracle that she ever survived birth for most of his babes were stillborn. She grew up, the only outward and visible sign of that first marriage of the King, a sour girl, with dark complexion, and spiteful eyes.

But the young Elizabeth was another story! She dared pull the royal whiskers, and tease him. Never for a moment was she afraid of him, toddling after him, and issuing demands, which, laughingly, he carried out for her. There was Edward, who became quite a strong little boy, after he recovered from a weak first month or so, grew some teeth, and put on fat. He was also the cleverest of the children, and, had he lived, would have been the most remarkable monarch. But death came too easily to a family frustrated by syphilis, and with that red cross chalked on the door of its life, almost before it ever began!

There was also the very pretty, very graceful little Lady Jane Grey, his favourite sister's grandchild, and Henry the Eighth had been devoted to Mary, when he was a boy.

But, whatever one may say, or what one

thinks of him, Henry the Eighth was the sour beast of the period. Crazy about display and all that it could give to him, mad on jewels, fine doublets and hose, and a man who *fought* for his own way, and dealt out death remorselessly. He was a despot, even to be his favourite friend meant it was time you sought a memorial stone for yourself! Growing older, and recognizing that he had never become the much admired young prince he once had hoped to be, he grew more sour, more ready to order torture, and death; yet throughout it all he nursed this contradictory kindly love for little children. It was the one white feather in his cap.

His own could do no wrong, save Mary (he admitted that they had never seen eye to eye, and never would), but Elizabeth and Edward and the little cousin, Mary's granddaughter, Jane, could tease him when that bad leg tortured him, and he accepted it.

'I adore children,' he said, and this was true.

At first, when Queen Jane died, he found himself with two daughters and a son, and believing that he could abandon 'wiving', and turn to fatherhood, so live the quieter life.

Henry suffered badly from false counsellors. Too many diarists forget to admit this. Then, when he had been gravely misled, he showed his shattering wrath in the most outrageous manner. Traitor's Gate, Tyburn, the block and the torturers. He had not wished to marry yet again, but his faithful advisers sought this, believing it would keep him in a more amiable mood, for none (who knew His Grace) could ever have agreed that he was the most amiable of men; he dealt out death, as most men deal out playing cards, when in a friendly game.

He was completely happy when with his children, and playing with them was something of which he never tired. Had all those stillborn babes which poor Katherine of Aragon bore him, survived and lived he would have been blissfully happy with them. But fate and the sins of the father beset him. He knew the malady which had killed his brother, Arthur, and his father in the early fifties. He had watched them die. Perhaps because he was young, and particularly strong, he believed that he had the power to fell this enemy, which in the end killed him, also!

He would have said that he had known more happiness with his children than with anyone else in this world, save perhaps the Princess Mary whom he had never cared for. But the young Duke of Richmond who had died of the malady which would kill his father, the sturdy, red-headed little Elizabeth, and the fat Prince of Wales were all his children and he played valiantly with them.

To the court there came frequently little Jane Grey. She was the granddaughter of the king's favourite sister, Mary of Suffolk, and this little family were more or less brought up together.

'It is right for children to be happy,' said this outrageously contradictory King, with the red beard and hair, and the flashing blue eyes which could go the colour of steel. He had, at one time, thought of little Jane, as being a suitable wife for his only son and a future Queen. The two words Queen Jane were engraven on his heart, for the real love of the eighth Henry lay buried with Jane Seymour in Windsor, as he knew well. He still loved the very name.

Even if he had re-married after dear Jane's death, it was because his advisers forced him. There had been the strange marriage to Anne of Cleves, who, in the end, became the most reliable of the first five wives, in that she could amuse him by cheating at cards, taking strange bets with him, and making him laugh! There had been the last wild impetus of love within him, when he saw the black-eyed little Kathryn Howard, had heard her girlish laughter, admiring her nimbleness, and had she not promised him the reward of a return of youth? She had almost succeeded too, for she got him back into the saddle, a great big, burly man, today a lump, not a rider, and his horse aching under him. But it had not lasted. She had died as the other dark-eyed Queen, her kinswoman, had done, and now Henry seldom went down to Hampton Court Palace, on an autumn eve, lest he should hear her voice, screaming, 'Henry?

Henry?' through the corridors.

His last wife was, of course, his best wife, if one who had never physically *been* his wife could say this. She cared for him, saw to his nauseous wounds, kept him to his diet (and he squirmed from it), and treated him more as matron than as wife.

But he could trust her.

None would ever poison him, whilst Katherine Parr was there to guard him and guard him she would.

'The children...' he would say.

Mary was adult now, and it had been Jane Seymour, the good and the just, who had brought her back to the palace to live with them.

Inwardly a rebel, he felt sure, for she was as strong a Catholic as had ever lived, and would die one! He prayed that he had made his own Church strong enough to resist her. He was sure that he had done all that he could! Mary would have brought back Catholicism, he knew that, but Mary would not reign. He had a son. A son of his own body, the boy whom Jane had given to him.

As he lay sick at Hampton, with that wicked throbbing in his leg, he watched the children playing on the lawns, and in the Queen's Garden. Red-headed Elizabeth (a firebrand, he told himself, and laughed to think that she had hair the same colour as his own). Edward, his nurse for ever minding him, for no harm must come to this most blessed heir, and Jane Grey, his great-niece! How good she was to the Prince of Wales!

'One day you will wed,' he told the girl, when they tired of playing, and came to him to sit with him.

'And then I shall have children of my own,' she said, and laughed.

'You could be Queen of England,' he said watching her with those small, foxy eyes of his, tremulously blue at times.

'I am not good enough,' she said.

She was a demure child. From her earliest days she had been surrounded by her teachers, and forced to work at her lessons. The education of a girl in her position was important. She was of the blood royal, and the part which she would play in life could easily be that of a queen! Perhaps it *was* as a queen that King Henry the Eighth thought of her!

'Learn your books, and do as your tutors tell you, Jane,' he told her.

'I will indeed, dear Uncle.'

He encouraged the children to play together. Now, in the final years of his life ('the mouldering years' he called them when in his deepest misery), he made happy plans for these children; plans which brought joy back into his heart, plans which could bring prosperity to the country, so he prayed. If Edward did espouse the young Lady Jane, it would be an agreeable alliance, which surely would help the country?

The children had always cared for one another, and had seen a lot of each other! The two older girls he felt, were apart—Mary he had actually disliked! He would never have come to care for her, had it not been for the care and goodness of his dear Jane, the wife who had died for him, in childbirth. Jane had brought Mary back into his home, insisting that, as the King's daughter, she had a right there!

Jane had always been the peacemaker, he knew that. God rest her soul. But somehow he felt sure that Jane would have been enchanted that her son espoused young Jane Grey, his dearest sister's grandchild, the little girl who had shared the royal nurseries at times, and who had always had an affectionate place in his heart.

The plans were going ahead for the alliance.

When the young prince was twelve years old, would be an agreeable moment for the alliance to be announced, and the two of them brought together. They had known one another all their lives. The girl was pretty, never beautiful, as some of Henry's wives had been (Anne Boleyn for instance, and the naughty little Kathryn Howard) but she had a good skin, was not pock-marked as were so many girls of her age, (her cousin, the Princess Mary, for instance) clear blue eyes, and darkish hair.

'One day you shall wed my son,' the old King told her, for, although in years, King Henry the

VIIIth was not old, but he had lived a dozen extra years in loose living, in eating and drinking, and spending a dangerous life. Ageing before his time, the disease which had so mercilessly destroyed his father, would end his life and when the hour came it ended the life of his children. The court was infected with it.

The hour came when, his condition rapidly worsening and the end obviously not far away, and Queen Katherine caring for him. Now he saw less and less of his children, and his favourite little great-niece Jane. A death chamber was no playground for the young, and Katherine sent them to Edgware.

The King spoke to her.

He said, 'When I go, too many will want the crown, and Edward *is* the king! Thank God, I have lived long enough to have that scheming Surrey beheaded, and the Duke of Norfolk shall die before the month is out.'

It was the king who died, Norfolk lived!

Henry the Eighth died soon after midnight on the morning of the 28th of January 1547. His widow wept for him, for she had worked hard during these years of marriage, and had dedicated herself to him. Now she heard the cry, 'The King is dead. Long live the King.' It was she who sent for the new King to be brought to the Palace of Whitehall, as soon as possible. She knew that the Duke of Northumberland plotted with the Lady Jane's father to gain the throne for the family, she *knew* life was dangerous.

★   ★   ★

The last time Edward had seen his father had been three whole weeks previously when the King's physicians had said that he was dying and he and Elizabeth had been sent away. The King had argued that he needed to have his son with him, but his wife was determined that the boy was too young. He must be spared the cold horror of death.

How furious His Grace had been. There had been a time when a flash of his heavy hand, would send food and golden vessels of wine crashing to the floor, in a hideous mêlée, which was disastrous! But his temper had never upset his sixth queen; she always waited until his breath gave out, and then said, 'This is not the way that Kings should behave!'

Recovering, he gasped, 'I could have sent you to The Tower of London for this, Madam,' and growled like some old lion!

He was never to see his son again! Perhaps in all his life that boy meant the most to him. He had waited so long for a male heir, he had been so proud of his brains, his calm, and his understanding. But now, in the last hours of his life, his mind wandered as death tapped on the door of his heart, seeking admittance.

He worsened suddenly.

January was running out! It had been a hard month, with sharp frosts, and it was now months since the fires in Whitehall Palace had been put out. 'The children, where are they?' he asked.

At Edgware, he was told. 'Why is not Jane with us? I miss Jane. She is nice to play with.'

Then came the call for them.

The end came fast. Earlier in the evening Henry had spoken of his widow going to the 'Dower Palace', which he had had built for her in Chelsea, and where she would live after his death until the dread messenger came for her in his own time. Then he lost consciousness.

They sat on either side of the bed, in the stuffy room into which not a single whiff of fresh air had penetrated for months. The huge fireplace was heaped with grey ashes and smelt of it. Every little while men servants brought in a fresh log, and placed it on the iron 'dogs', and they could hear the sap oozing out of it, and sizzling against the flames.

The aged Cranmer came to him.

Possibly he knew full well that this would be the last time that his overbearing master sent for him! It had been a difficult service that he had fulfilled, intensely hard, and how he had kept his head he would never know! He had seen too many good men and women go to the block, or to bloody Tyburn, and had half-expected to end his days at one or the other himself. It was a hard world!

He looked at the sick man, who failed to recognize him. 'His Grace is failing?' he asked the Queen.

She nodded, her eyes full of tears for she was a kind woman, a woman who had always wept to see her husband die, even this the hardest man of them all.

'It cannot be long, he needs prayer,' was what she whispered.

Beside the bed, with its evil-smelling linen, and that suppurating leg, which was killing him, and which stunk to high Heaven, Cranmer made a desperate attempt to solicit the aid of the Almighty! When he had done, he asked questions.

'The little King?'

'If he were awakened now, he could not get here in time,' said his step-mother, 'and I do not want the child bewildered by the panoply of death. He is so young.'

'Death comes to all men,' said the Archbishop, pompously.

She knew that, but because she loved children dearly, she would have kept the misery of it from this child's eyes. 'The King has not another hour to live, the boy would not be here in time, and if he came, His Grace would not know him! It would be sad for him to see his father like this,' and she said it in the way which meant she was having no interference. Within minutes the end came. She saw her husband die, and closed his eyes, tears in her own, for strangely enough this woman loved him.

'You will send for the children?' Cranmer asked her.

'I shall send for them immediately.'

The King is dead, long live the King, she was saying to herself. She went to her room, her step-daughter with her, for now, when there was no need to be brave any further, she could commit herself to the tears she had held back so courageously all along. She had already despatched a messenger to Edgware.

What she did not know in that hour, was that nothing was going to work out the way that the late King had wished, and which she herself desired for the boy King. Foreseeing the disaster of everybody fighting to be Regent for the boy king, his late Majesty had left the Regency to a body of sixteen members, with the Earl of Hertford, uncle of the heir to the crown, as their chief. He would never know that almost immediately Seymour, (unscrupulous as they come, and designing) made himself Protector of the Realm, and of the King's purpose, and gave himself the Dukedom of Somerset.

There was to be no 'middle course' to the Anglo-Catholic faith, which the King had mapped out, and had ordained. It was the Duke of Somerset who, within but a few hours, flung himself into the hands of the Protestants, and swept aside those few remnants of the old faith, which even King Henry had thought wise to retain. He had sought that the service kept its original form of being read in Latin, but it was Somerset who instantly abolished this.

As the coach with the royal children in it, bowled along the road towards the Palace of Whitehall, where the dead king lay, the faith of England was changing completely!

Disaster lay ahead.

PART ONE

THE LITTLE LADY JANE GREY

Remove not the ancient landmark.
Wm. Shakespeare

ONE

> A little rule, a little sway.
> A sunbeam on a winter's day,
> As all the proud and mighty have
> Between the cradle and the grave.
>
> Cornger Hill

IN the July of 1543 the dark-eyed Lady Latymer, twice widowed already, and still in the early twenties, married again. She was wretchedly poor! She had accepted a post at court, for the salary it gave her, and had but two gowns to take with her. Now she wedded yet again, the third oldish man. The bridegroom was King Henry the Eighth, and they plighted their troths in the Queen's Closet at Hampton Court.

The new Queen was much the same age as the King's elder daughter, the Princess Mary, the only living child of poor Katherine of Aragon. Curiously enough, the two got on well together, though it would be extremely difficult for anyone to have fallen out with so sweet a lady as the thrice-wedded Queen Katherine.

Lord Latymer had died six months previously, and the poor lady needed employment which actually gave her food, and the palace had a good name for generosity when it came to this. Henry the Eighth had never been a gentleman who wasted time; he was lonely; he had been deeply hurt by the break of his marriage with that little minx Kathryn Howard, and he needed some kind woman who could comfort him.

He had noticed her when she first came to his court, a very dark woman with languorous dark eyes, which attracted him. He saw in her a good mother for his children, a wise housewife, she was not irritated easily, and she never showed bad temper. Also she was an excellent nurse (his own doctors had told him so), and the hour had come when these were—alas!—the main conveniences that marriage could give to him. A homely woman, and kind. A good nurse.

Gone were those gay days when he had romped to the marriage bed, and had laughed at the thought that the pageboys had their eyes to the keyholes, and the chatter below stairs later, would be something for all to hear. He sought a good wife, and a sweet woman; he wanted a mother for his children, a companion for his old age, and someone who could soothe that infernal leg of his, and save him sometimes from that infernal stinging pain that it offered to him.

She gave him all these things!

She was almost the same age as his elder daughter, and sought to be the children's mother, rather than his wife. She had always adored babes, was concerned for the health of the young prince, who needed great care and attention. She was accepted gallantly at court, and made friends with all who met her, in particular, with Mary Tudor, the daughter of the late King, Henry the Seventh, and *this* Henry's sister. Mary was the grandmother of little Lady Jane Grey.

'I can trust my granddaughter with you,' Mary told the new Queen.

She met little Jane Grey when she was about five years old, a charming girl, simple and obedient, and, so the teachers said, a brilliant scholar. It was Queen Katherine who had suggested to the King that Lady Jane Grey came more frequently to the palaces, and did her lessons with the little prince. Vying one with another was encouraging. The King agreed, and Jane was his favourite niece.

'She shall live here as much as she can,' he agreed.

Little Lady Jane had been born near Leicester, in the year 1537, which had been about the time when Henry was making plans to rid himself of the German bride whom he had married because the picture he had seen of her fascinated him. Today Anne of Cleves, divorced and in the background of his life, came to festivities, amiably enough, and never worried anyone! She had quaint foibles. She brought a special bag, in which she took home with her pieces of food she could not eat then, but believed they might be useful later on! She never left a feast without pocketfuls of cakes and such.

England was passing through one of its more difficult periods of time. The Protestant faith was almost founded satisfactorily, and if nuns and monks begged in the gutters, or died in dark sheds, committing their souls to the Almighty and glad to go, on the whole one would have said that the Church of England was here! The new consort encouraged the joy of having the children at court with her. Now the old King was within sight of the end. Time was running out for him, and when the sharpness of winter came each year, he lost more strength and the race with death quickened.

The country waited for him to die, speculative as to what would happen. All manner of stories went the rounds. It was rumoured that, when young Edward had been born, seers had foretold that he would be a king, but never a crowned one! In the murky alleys off Bread Street, the stinking low water by the Thames itself, the houses of easy virtue, and the gambling booths, it was said that young Edward had the same disease, and would die before he could wed, or give the nation a Prince of Wales—or reign!

Now the King could live at the most but a few more months, and the Seymour family watched, speculating. They were ambitious. They had already burnt their fingers in far too many pies, and when this king died, there would be the proposition of the guardian of the young king until he came of age. Who *would* that be? That was where the future lay, of course.

A new year was about to be born. Since November Henry the Eighth had suffered wretchedly. Now it was dubious if he did not pray to go if only for freedom of that shattering pain which his body ever offered to him. With mid-January his condition had worsened.

The Queen had despatched the two younger children, Princess Elizabeth, and the Prince of Wales, to Edgware to stay. The rotten stench of sickness filled the palace, and sickened one. Katherine knew that death was close, and then one night she had a terrifying warning dream.

She thought that she saw the king himself, standing beside her bed radiant and wearing all his jewels, and instructing her to guard the young king with her own body, and love him for ever.

The strange thing was that very same night, Nurse Penn dreamt a similar dream and came weeping to the new step-mother. On the strength of this the Queen ordered the children away. It was wrong for the sweet brilliance of youth to be close to the cold horror of hard suffering, the shock of deep pain and what it could do to the human body, and the wretchedness of being unable to help! To make it easier for the two younger children Katherine asked little Jane Grey to go with them. The little prince adored Jane, she was a sympathetically kind child, who would do anything for another, and was goodness itself.

On the morning of the King's death, the Princess Elizabeth saw a vision, and told her brother that she was sure that her father was already dead. That morning the Protector himself came to them, despatched by the Queen, to bring them to the palace. As he approached Prince Edward, he gave that deep bow, that sweeping downwards which is kept only for the sovereign and the older sister recognized it.

He is already dead, she told herself, and clasped her cousin Jane's hand. The boy looked up.

'I pray that my father does not suffer,' he said.

'His Grace has suffered much, but it is better now,' was what was said.

'He is dead.' The Princess Elizabeth spoke calmly, and so somehow by the fact that none denied her, she knew that it was true.

The King had lost consciousness before midnight had struck, and had struggled to breathe. Cranmer had been with him at the end and his wife.

'I have been instructed to bring you to the Palace of Whitehall,' Seymour said.

The boy looked at him 'Jane, also?'

'The Lady Jane Grey also,' was the reply.

'I desire that she is with me,' said the new king, for she was more than sister to him, and much much more than cousin.

Young Edward had always disliked his elder sister, even when he was a babe in arms, and had screamed when he went to her. As a small child he had resented her ugliness, and her sharpness, the way she was ever ready to slap, and seldom to kiss! When he was sufficiently old enough to realize that all authority lay with him, and now, as king, he could command the court, he felt more sure of himself and less alarmed of her.

His old nurse wrapped him up in a heavy fur coat, for the day was sharp, and the roads rigid in a thick white frost. 'You will be a good king,' she said, 'and as a king you can do whatsoever you wish.'

He did not wish to be alone, and urged the others to travel with him. Possibly he was afraid of the unknown, and needed companions near his own age with him.

'Shall I have to do more lessons?' he asked Nurse Penn.

'It wouldn't surprise me, sire. All kings have to learn more than others.'

'But kings give orders.'

'*When* they grow up,' she said, 'as yet you are not grown up. You must remember that.'

★   ★   ★

He had indeed to learn more, for he was crammed mercilessly, morning, noon, and night. He had an aptitude for learning, which his father would have had, and benefited by, had he used it forcefully, but he was for ever dreaming of wine, women, and song, and never followed the right road through life.

Already the experience of the king's daughters had been strange; Mary had never forgiven him for divorcing her mother, and consigning her to outer darkness. She never would forgive it. A delicate girl she suffered from the most distressing migraines which ravaged her from time to time. Unattractive and intensely plain at a period of time when beauty was a female necessity, she had been soured by the horror of her own experiences, the annulment of her mother's marriage, and then the new wives who were for ever coming to the court. Though she had loved Jane Seymour, who had actually died in her arms, (she had also loved the last queen). But for Jane Seymour she kept the tenderest memory, for it was Jane who had insisted that the Princess come back to her own home to live. She had tamed the arbitrary demands of the obstreperous King, and had quite early in her marriage brought the elder princess to her right place at table, on the sovereign's right hand, and the younger girl to the other side of him. She had even insisted that his bastard boy, Henry Richmond come to live with them, a ghost boy, dying of the same complaint which, when the hour came, would kill the eighth Henry.

Anne of Cleves had never meant much to them, and all three children disliked Kathryn Howard who, poor girl, had been squirmed on to the consort's throne by her scheming Uncle Norfolk, and had lost her head because she had sought the crown.

Possibly the ageing Henry had married the Howard girl because she treated him as none of the others had done. She gave him back his youth. She persuaded him that he could dance, if he would but try, and he did try! He allowed himself to be hoisted into the saddle again and had ridden away to hunt in the forest. I *am* young again, he told himself, and believed that this girl still in her teens and lovely as a Tudor rose herself, could give him back life's richest asset, which is only lent to all of us for a few brief hours.

The royal children had known little of what was going on, for Nurse Penn was vigilant to keep scandal from them. The Prince of Wales was the apple of her eye, she never left him! She was particularly fond of little Lady Jane Grey.

She had always thought of the Princess Elizabeth as being something of a hoyden, and although good to her little brother, did not trust her completely. But it was Jane who played most frequently with him; who kissed the place to make it better, and comforted him when he fell, and hurt himself. 'I love Jane,' he once said, and his old nurse purred with her approval.

The whole family had gone down to Hampton Court Palace for the festival of All Saints. The servants were chattering, of course, for poignant rumours were going the rounds that the young Queen Kathryn (born a Howard) and young Tom Culpepper were having an affair! The old nurse shut the door of the Prince's nurseries on all such flippant chatter.

Then, in the middle of it all, after church on the morning of the day, the Queen disappeared. None saw her go. Few knew for certain that she *had* gone, but the rumour was going the round.

The King was in one of his most intolerable moods, saw nobody, and crashed about the palace like some young pugilist desiring to pick a fight. Then there came the news, that last night Culpepper had disappeared, and none knew whither. It meant that today the suppurating sore on the King's leg was giving him tremendous pain! None of his attendants could bind the wound as could young Culpepper, and tonight he was not in the palace! The old nurse closed fast the door of the nurseries, for whatever others said, they must say nothing before the children. *Nothing* she insisted, yet again.

Yet within a few more hours, all knew that

another of Henry the Eighth's unhappy wives had entered The Tower of London, passing under that despicable barrier known as Traitor's Gate, and that she would never see the light of day again! Nor Culpepper either.

'We are returning to London,' said the old nurse, and she took the children back with her.

Princess Elizabeth discovered what was going on, for she was one of those children with whom secrets availed nothing. She would search down to the last grain of dust, to discover what she thought was being said.

In these last years of his life the prematurely aged Henry became more and more impossible to understand. Now the rotting leg stank insufferably, almost asphyxiating those who nursed him. It was then that the Queen sent the children back to Edgware. She did not wish them to watch suffering and despair. They are the two visitors we all meet sooner or later, and, if anyone can postpone the meeting for us, that is the kind way.

'They are so young,' said the gentle queen, and the wisest of all his wives, of course. 'I would not wish them to suffer. Tell them that their father is not so well, and does not like noise. Tell them he must rest. Let the bad news come to them gently.'

★   ★   ★

On that cold January morning, the messenger came before the light to send for them. The boy must come to Whitehall immediately, no longer as the Prince of Wales, but as the King of England, and he and his sister, and Jane, went back together.

'I want Jane to be with me,' he said.

'Then she shall come,' said the old nurse, and she told the men to drive fast. They travelled through wild country, the trees skeletons, the branches making sounds like whips as they struck the cold air in the wind. They came down the hill into the village of Hampstead, and on past farmhouses, and an occasional cottage, into London itself. The bells were tolling. They made a dismal enough sound echoing over dismal London, the city perched on a hill, then the break of the occasional field, and the river Fleet on one side, and the river Thames on the other. Approaching closer Whitehall Palace, the noise of the bell in the Abbey became insistent and strong.

The little boy stared out of the window. 'Listen to the bells tolling,' he said.

It was little Jane Grey who said piously, 'When the hour comes, we all have to go, but when all bells toll, then it is crowned head that has gone.'

Instantly, the old nurse took his hand and comforted him with that tender ability of hers which she had used since she first took him newly-born to her bosom, and whispered, 'A King for England! God be praised! We must accept God's will,' was what she told him.

The coach turned, rattling into the courtyard of Whitehall Palace itself, and instantly the grooms who had been awaiting the arrival came forward and placed the steps to the door. Several people moved to greet the King. My Lord Cranmer spoke first, his eyes kind, his voice ageing now, inclined to flicker.

'Your Grace,' he said, and gave the royal bow, deep down, and unhurried.

'My—my father is really dead?'

'Your father is dead, Sire,' and then quietly. 'This is the hour when you have good advisers waiting to assist your Grace.'

Little Jane Grey was being helped out of the difficult coach, and a flunkey lifted her right down. The young King put out a hand to her. 'I want Jane to be with me.'

For the moment these men, and not all of them true friends, would agree to anything that he said, but the old woman, who had first held him in her kind arms at birth, watched them going, distrustful of their urbanity, and not sure. She clicked her teeth together, teeth long and still strong as horses are! 'Tst. Tst,' she said.

She followed, as closely as she dared, weeping slightly. He would she knew, be a good king, but he was very young, and she prayed that they would let her stay near him. Until this moment she had done everything for him, and she was perhaps, the only person in all this wide world whom he could trust! He still was troubled by nightmares at times, and would wake screaming. He was not shy, but well spoken, and he had sudden premonitions of an approaching danger, a danger others could not see. As she stepped down the last stair of the ladder to the earth, the boy stopped and turned back to her.

'Penny? I want Penny?'

'Your Grace is now too old for nurses.'

He stopped dead, and drew himself up to his full height. 'If I am the King of England, as you tell me, it is I who give the orders. My people who obey me.'

'But Your Grace...?'

'I give the orders,' he said, and turned again to the nurse. She struggled to him, as fast as rheumy knees would permit, and bobbed him a curtsey. 'We will find your step-mother, Sire,' she promised him.

They entered the palace together, the others glancing at one another, for this could not continue. They entered the exquisite palace of Whitehall which his father had snatched from poor Cardinal Wolsey, with all its precious collections, and had won his second wife's heart by loading her with the remarkable treasures which it contained. The guard saluted. That was when the boy recognized finally that Edward the Prince, was no more. It was King Edward the Sixth who entered his own home!

TWO

> After death shall we sleep? Why, souls do not sleep, even when are alive; it is only the body that sleeps.
> *Tertullian*, A.D. *200*

THE child who had driven up to the palace with his playmate and his old nurse, felt himself terribly alone. He went on ahead, but little Jane Grey hesitated.

'It is all right,' said the nurse, 'I am here,' and she took the girl into a small side room. The strange part of Whitehall Palace was that very few of its rooms were really spacious, and this was quite a tiny room, a log fire crackling on its hearth and the stench of wood smoke, of ashes, and of human sweat everywhere.

'We will wait instructions here,' she suggested, 'the Queen will wish to see you, but we must be very quiet, for death is with us,' she gave her hand to the child. So they sat there patiently, the strong smoky atmosphere bringing tears into their eyes, and every now and then a gust of wind sending a great belching cloud of it back into the room!

'Nobody has come to us,' said the child, at last, 'Do you suppose that they have forgotten that we are here?'

'No, they must be very busy! We have to wait.'

In the end it was one of the Queen's own ladies who came for them. Strangely enough, poor Queen Katherine had been very distressed by the loss of her husband, for whom she had cared quite deeply. She had of course, never been in love with him (that one understood) but he was her child, the man whose pain she sought to save, and who, in his better moments, had thanked her for all that she did. The lady brought the two of them into the Queen's presence. Katherine was dressed in sombre black, and wore no jewels at all, but she opened her arms wide to the little girl.

'Jane ... Jane, my dear,' she gasped. And then. 'Edward came with you, surely? Where is he?'

'His relations met Edward,' Jane curtseyed delicately to the Queen, then went closer to kiss hands, and instantly was clasped to her breast. One of the loveliest and most remarkable points about the Queen was the fact that she was always exactly the same. 'My Uncle ... ?' she asked.

'It was for the best, for he suffered terribly the last few weeks, and he endured it so bravely.' The Queen checked her own tendency to weep, and the little girl saw that her cheeks were swollen with spent tears. In the background, for the first time, she recognized that her cousin the Princess Mary was there. She and Mary had never really got on together but very few people *did* get on with this princess, though her tender care for the Queen was remarkable and always had been.

'Madam ... it is for the best...' the child whispered.

'I know. It is God's will! He is our king,' and the poor girl wiped her eyes again.

The child asked, 'Where will His Grace rest for ever?'

'He made me promise some time ago that he should rest in Windsor, in the chapel there beside the mother of his son.' The poor Queen wished that she could prevent the tears from rising, but they came involuntarily. In her own strange way, she had loved him, but more as a mother loves her son, than as a woman cares for her husband! They had never been husband and wife of course, she admitted that, but, in name only, she was his queen.

Perhaps now when the hour had come, part of her longed to retire to the palace which he had built for superfluous queens, as some rude counsellor had once said. She would return to the Chelsea Dower House with its large, quiet garden and the other side of the hawthorn hedge, the big river itself, with its steady flow and ships passing to and fro on it.

And there, as she had always planned, Tom Seymour (now returned to England) would act as her steward, and run the place for her. For a single moment her heart missed a beat and although thrice married, she had never felt this loving thrilling emotion.

This queen, Henry's last one, had held this secret for ever hidden in her heart. None knew of it, and at this particular time there were no rumours, no disquiet, no chat. She sought to go now to her own palace, the one which Henry had always promised should be her own.

'You will live here, Madam?' Jane asked her.

'No. No, not here. This is the King's own house, and he will need it. I shall go to live in the Dower House, the Queen's Dower House, which His Grace had built for me in Chelsea.'

The child looked at her, her blue eyes brimming over with tears, for this had been the most difficult morning of her life. 'If I could come with you, Madam...? If you would let me stay with you, as I have done before?'

The kind Queen took the child's hand, and smoothed its softness with her own be-ringed fingers, 'My dear, I have always been the stepmother of the King's children. Mary is my friend, Edward is, as my own son would have been, and I adore little Elizabeth, even when she is so naughty (and she can be very naughty indeed).' She hesitated. 'If your people will permit it, my child, then you shall come with me.' She stayed her tears, and spoke on in a firmer voice. 'My little sweetheart, listen to me. The King loved you more than any other of his relatives, and you know this. There is a rumour that your marriage, when the hour comes, could bring you to the throne itself! If that is what is to be, then I for one desire it.'

The child put her arms about the kind lady's neck, and kissed her tenderly, 'I dare not even think of it,' she confessed, and the colour sped into her face. 'Oh Madam, how much I desire to be with you!'

The Queen embraced her with fervour, a bigly-made, affectionate woman, a born mother at heart. They sat there talking for some time, none interrupting them, and then the new King himself had asked to come to them. Two gentlemen would have accompanied him, but he sent them back from the very threshold.

'I am my own master,' he said, and held out his hand to be kissed by his little playmate.

'Sire,' she said, and he put his arms closer about her, and drew her up to her feet again.

'Nothing shall alter our friendship,' he said. 'Never leave me Jane. Never.'

His stepmother said, 'Jane is coming to live with me at the Dower Palace, beside Chelsea Reach, and you can visit her whenever you desire. I want your happy friendship to endure.'

The boy nodded, then went closer to her. 'I am hungry! We had but half our breakfast for they were so anxious to start for London, and I want food! I want also to see my sisters. I want *you*.'

Instantly, this kind sweet woman who had always done so much for the King's children, and his great-niece, put an arm round the boy. She had hot food brought for him, and she herself took the children to see the dead King.

It would not have been proper if this visit had been omitted. Even the quite small children of the period came to view the dead; she knew. She insisted that they did not go too close to the corpse, for now there was the almost unbearable stench, which death had magnified, and made even more repulsive! His baldness showed badly. It was something that he had ever hidden under a dark velvet-tasselled cap, over which he could place other caps.

'Do not go closer,' their stepmother said, her eyes wet, and her heart ached with despair, for she had endured so much for this one man. In death he had changed considerably. He seemed to be much taller; ever a great man (his measurements were six foot, four inches in height) now he seemed to be even taller. They stood just inside the doorway, no nearer.

'This is your good-bye to him,' she whispered, and she knew that Henry had, in some ways, been a noble father; he would have done anything for his children.

'Can I live in the Dower Palace with you?' the little King asked her seriously.

'No, Edward. I do not think that will be possible, for the Sovereign's place is either at St. James, or in Whitehall; but you *must* remember that my door is for ever open to you; The Dower Palace shall be your second home. Come and go there as you wish.'

'I like its name,' said Jane, 'The Dower Palace, and there we *are* safe?'

'Quite safe,' the Queen promised them.

Only the matter of days later, she moved into the Dower Palace, taking with her all her few, precious belongings, and, in a way, she was glad to go! She had never liked the atmosphere of the Palace of Whitehall, once Cardinal Wolsey's priceless home, and annexed by the late King. He had gone over it, surprised by the rich hangings, the gold and silver exposed there, clever furniture and tapestries (it must have cost the Cardinal a fortune) and the King had shown it to Anne Boleyn, at the time his own love!

Now she made alterations, for she had never been one of those quietly gentle women who do not appreciate rich hangings, jewelled fireplaces and such. She made it a warmly comfortable house, where children could play if they wished, and kings come for comfort.

She was particularly pleased with the garden, which ran down to the river. She had stood at the window watching the tides passing her by, much as life had done! She had been wived three times, and yet was still a virgin. Now all that was past. This home she could run as she pleased, and Tom Seymour was to be her *Major Domo*.

I love him, she thought, yet was half ashamed when but so recently widowed, she could still think fondly of the man.

She had married three husbands, and each of them had been old men. She was the type of woman who liked youth, and the joys that it can bring. Standing at her own window, and looking out across the water to the village of Battersea, she thought of youth as being nothing more or less than a vagrant escort! When we are very young, we think that it is worthless, but times change for us.

She went, of course, to the King's funeral at Windsor, the one mourner who walked directly behind the heir, the little king, and she conducted herself magnificently.

'God sends us life for the best,' she thought, 'and maybe this will work out for the best for me.'

But she wondered!

The new little King cast down earth into the vault, where his poor mother also lay, paying the heavy price of giving a King to England. The boy King dribbled a little earth on to the coffin lid, from the big silver spoon kept for this purpose. I pray for him, was what he thought, but he felt as if a ghost plucked at his sleeve, and this was not true. His father had been too big and strong to die!

I pray for the boy, his stepmother thought.

He hated the ceremony and the melancholy and then he caught sight of the bright eyes of his little cousin Jane Grey. They walked out of the chapel together, and over to the palace. Coming into the garden he asked his stepmother to walk with them for he loved her.

'I want you,' he said, 'I want you to be with me for ever. You have always been wonderful to me.'

Behind them walked the Princess Mary, and with her the younger Princess Elizabeth. Young Edward felt that Elizabeth was nearer to his stepmother than others of the family. Yet in his personal life he had come to the parting of the ways. Kings walk alone, and he would do this for all the time ahead. When the hour came that he wedded, then his wife would be the nearest friend he had in all his life. I *must* marry, he told himself, and this not only because there must be heirs to follow me to the Stone of Scone, but because I need companionship.

They went into the castle to take food. They talked of the future and Edward spoke of the time when he would have children, too.

'All sons,' he said and laughed, 'all must be boys. I shall will that, for I want heirs. I need at least three to follow after me,' and he laughed.

They walked later into the private garden, where already there were thick buds on the branches, and the aconites coming out in cups of gold. The shoemack trees were bright (they leaf young), but the chrysanthemums had now faded. The boy and girl were together.

He said, 'What lies ahead for us, Jane dear?'

'I know not, my Lord.'

'I desire to marry you when the hour comes, you know that, don't you? I would promise to give you happiness.'

'I know,' she said, 'but somehow I have the feeling that it is not for me.'

'But this is the springtime of your happiness,' he said.

'It is still winter,' she whispered, sadly, 'I have always believed I'd die young, and horribly. I—I shall lose my head.'

Horrified he said, and sternly, 'But never that.'

She whispered. 'Poor, poor Queen Anne, Elizabeth's mother, and poor Queen Kathryn, her stepmother; both of them died at The Tower, kneeling before a block,' and she shuddered.

'But not you! Those days are over for ever, for I will abolish death as a punishment, I will have none of it,' he said.

'Alas, death is necessary to this hard world, for dead men tell no tales,' and he saw that her cheeks were wet.

He turned, and kissed her, as he had often done before, from the time he was a baby in a pram. His voice was sad, 'I would end fighting, and war and horror. I would end death, if I could. What I am going to ask for in my reign is peace.'

A man came out of the door to the palace, approaching them quietly, stopping to bow and then coming nearer. 'It is Sir Thomas Seymour who would have a word with the Lady Jane Grey,' he said quietly.

'What could he want?' the King asked.

'It is cold out here, after all, it is still winter, maybe he brings me a cloak or something?' and she went towards the castle. Edward went with her. He had the idea that they had already gone a long way into the future hand-in-hand.

THREE

O Englishmen!—in tongue and creed,
In blood and tongue our brothers!
We too, are heirs of Runnymede,
And Shakespeare's name, and Cromwell's dead,
    Are not alone our mother's.
                John Green Leaf Whittier

THE child Jane grew up rapidly, for the circumstances under which she lived, ordained this. She was extremely happy when staying with the dowager queen in the Dower Palace, for she adored Katherine, who was kindness itself to her.

Like many others she did not get on well with the Princess Mary constantly visiting there and very fond of the Queen Mother, but she liked Princess Elizabeth, a tomboy of a girl, excitable, giddy and emphatic in everything that she did, and she sought to live life more as a man than as a woman. She rode well, could duel, though this was denied her.

The nation settled down after the death of a King who had almost ruined them with his extravagances, and who had destroyed their faith putting the new one in its place. They were glad to see him go, and looked with pride at the boy king, who succeeded him! But the boy looked ill! Was he as strong as men said? Soon after his father's death, he had been laid low with a most vehement cold (probably pneumonia) which he could not shake off properly.

It would be some time before he would wed, and give the country an heir of course, but he was a clever lad, had all his father's brains, and none of that licentiousness it seemed, which the late Henry had possessed so freely.

The seers declared that the king would never mature sufficiently to wed, and that he would have no children! A woman would come next to the throne! In truth there were several candidates. First and foremost the daughter of Katherine of Aragon, the Princess Mary. It is true that she had been bastardized by her own father, when his marriage to her mother had become a difficult bond which he desired to sever. The same thing had happened with that red-headed sister of hers, by far the cleverest and most determined of them all.

The powers-that-be knew that it was desirable for the king to marry very young, and the sooner the better. Behind him now stood two bastardized sisters, his cousin, the wife of the French Prince, Mary (who became Mary, Queen of Scots), and little Jane Grey.

By the time that Easter came, people had become used to the fact that the old king was dead. They awaited the excitement of the new May Day. It was, of course, well known that the little king's uncles were arguing together, for the palace was a chaos of intrigue.

The Queen Dowager had moved into the Dower Palace, and found it amiable and comfortable, with a glorious garden and new fruit trees everywhere promising a wonderful summer ahead of them. It was pleasant to be away from the turmoil of the streets she told herself, nice to be here with the happy children under her wing, and not that demanding and petulant invalid continuously shrieking her name.

He had been the demanding invalid, as he had been the demanding king, wanting all at once! Scandals went the rounds of course. Would his widow wed yet again? and men and women sniggered in the taverns as they thought of it. Whom would the Princess Elizabeth wed for she was approaching the age when one thought of a husband for her. Some chattered of Seymour, who had an appointment with the widowed queen as guardian of her home, high steward, whatever he wished to call himself, but some said that he had his eyes on the queen herself as a bride! She would be rich. She still had a certain dark beauty of her own, although already thrice wed.

The chatter grew.

The time came when it was the talk of London, for this poor lady (who had already been wed three times) was said to love Seymour, to submit to his sometimes coarse teasings (for he had a vulgar tongue when loosened) and made ready, possibly she was a little attracted, for this was the first time that she had had a young man in the house with her. All her three husbands had been old men, with death for ever knocking on their door of life. She knew this. She had never married for love.

Now with the children, and often little Jane Grey with her, she thought of love again. She liked the new Lord Admiral as he was called, and tried to hide her feelings from him.

The Lord Admiral did make the suggestion that the Princess Elizabeth, approaching years of discrimination, could be a bride, but although a dazzling figure of a man, the suit was not favoured. Elizabeth disliked men, she said. She was a tomboy of a girl, loved horses, and riding, would have played men's games, had it been allowed, and the court chattered about her. The King was not yet cold in his grave at Windsor, and some said that the dowager Queen was considering re-marriage. The most scandalized person was, of course, the Princess Mary!

'Something should be done, or some law made,' she declared, her eyes dark with fury, 'to save my stepmother from this scandalous marriage. She has had three husbands and one of them a king! I know my father had six wives, but he needed a queen to share the heavy burden on his shoulders! She needs none to share her burden.'

And, it was spring again!

It was a warm and lovely spring, when the cowslips came early, smelling like new milk in the meadows, whilst in competition the hedges smelt like wine with the abundance of the blossom on the thorn. It was a very beautiful spring, born early in April with the wild violets and the cuckoo flowers everywhere. For the first time poor Katherine, Henry's sixth Queen, was feeling the comfort of freedom, of being alone, of being her own mistress. And Seymour was near her!

It is possible that the poor lady was in love with youth; it could so easily have happened to her, after three old husbands.

Now she lived in her own home, with an ideal garden, and the Thames running past the windows. Elizabeth was with her, very often Jane as well, and she was a lady who loved children. It was cruel that she had never had a child of her own!

It is fairly plain that this poor lady, who had behaved with the greatest heroism in her devotion to the late King and untiring efforts on his behalf, now came into her own springtime! Married the first time at but seventeen, she had never had any girlhood at all herself, and had lived under immense strain! But, from her late 'teens, she had admired and loved Seymour! This was but natural in one so deprived. He was a plotter. Possibly even in that early hour to men who knew, the young king's health was a matter of private consternation. Perhaps he realized the boy would never become a man, and then a woman would be in power! He had tried for Elizabeth, and had been repulsed. He did not hang back. Born a schemer (a man who was determined to fight for what he wanted) he had looked again. Mary no one would want. Elizabeth he could not have, but Katherine was a trained queen. Katherine would without doubt receive him, if for nought else, because she had been starved of human emotion.

The first time he kissed her, he must have tasted her hunger for happiness. He must have known.

London was preparing for the May Day Revels. It had been such a truly beautiful spring, so many flowers, such sweet singing, and the very spirit of the occasion everywhere. The old King's death was slipping into the past, and now the young king was popular. Spring *is* the hour of love, as all the world knows.

The first chatter started in the back alleys of London, down on the wharfs (or by the river Fleet, lying low because there had been so little rain, and smelling foully, while the last of Henry's wives arranged her dark hair more becomingly, and found herself humming the May songs. It was noticed.

The palaces were all hotbeds of chatter, and the news gained speed as it went along its route. The couple were being careful, but not sufficiently so. The child Jane was with them (Katherine's favourite of them all, it was known) and she really loved this gentle little girl. She was interested also in her tremendous progress with her tutors, and instructors. Her Latin and French were superb, she had always read like a glutton, one day she would be a very brilliant woman, that was obvious. She had been fond of the King's daughters, Princess Mary, as though she were a sister, Princess Elizabeth, a naughty tomboy, of course, but like her own child! Here was joy in her own palace, the one that the King had bequeathed to her, and where she could be so happy, and perhaps forget some of the horrors which had already menaced her, horrors that she would rather forget, poor thing, but she wanted to keep little Jane Grey with her.

There had been the night, the formidable night when she had fallen into an uneasy sleep, and when half-awake from it, had dreamt a terrible dream. Of herself dying here in this very palace! Of Elizabeth in a barge going down the Thames, to where lies the dark doorway to the prison of The Tower and known as Traitor's Gate, stood open to receive her. Worse still, of Jane, walking like a queen, quietly and slowly, pale as death itself, and death waiting to meet her on the scaffold that she approached; the scaffold where *other* queens had died. The names were written on her heart. Anne Boleyn. Kathryn Howard.

She woke with a scream.

She sat up in bed, clutching at her hair, and her ears, and weeping bitterly. In this hour, the very hour when she had tonight planned her secret marriage with Seymour. This month. This happy, happy month when May Queens were crowned and love was everywhere!

It isn't true, she told herself, clasping her face and trying to control her tears. Whatever happened she did not want others to know of what was going on. She must control herself. Somehow.

I dream too much, she thought. I dream too much. I should think of marriage again. I should not disturb myself with dreams. My duty here is to guard the King's children, and little Jane. To make young Edward fit for the future, which will be his mighty job. For, whatever else he did, he must establish the new Church. She had promised on the Bible, and holding her husband's hand with hers, that, whatever else she did, she would see that the Church *was* established. The young King was anxious for it. Elizabeth wanted it, but Mary bitterly resented it, and when she was in this mood, Mary was the most cruel enemy of them all.

Whatever happened, the Dowager Queen, in her own palace, prayed for the future. She had promised her husband before he died, that she would do what he sought from her, and she *would* do it, for Katherine was a woman of her word. She tried to check memories of life with Henry which had, at times, been close to the unbearable, and she told herself that she must keep her promises.

The little King must live.

He must live long enough to grow up, and to marry Jane. That was her dream for him. He must last long enough to give Jane a son, a boy who would exclude for ever from the throne, the

Princess Mary. If she came to the Stone of Scone, Katherine shivered for the fighting that there would be, the bloodshed and tortures, of men—and women also—dying for their faith. Edward would marry Jane, she promised herself, and they must have a son to make the future secure!

It is only a matter of a few more years, she told herself as she thought about it, wandering in the pretty Knot Gardens of her own palace. But have I got those few more years? she asked herself.

FOUR

> We are such stuff
> As dreams are made on, and our little life
> Is rounded with a sleep.
> *Wm. Shakespeare*

IN the next few months little Lady Jane Grey spent quite a lot of time with the Dowager Queen, and was very happy to be with her.

The Dower Palace was far more pleasant than anywhere else where they had lived hitherto, and the child was enchanted by its beauty, and the lovely flowers which grew in the comfortable gardens. It was one of the more curious characteristics of the departed King Henry, that he had such a surprising admiration for flowers, and ordered that some of them must be for ever near to him.

Undoubtedly, Henry the Eighth was a man who had several sides to his nature, for although in many ways he was little less than a monster, in others he was agreeable, amiable and royal. He adored children and, in their turn, they all loved him. He ordered that wherever he stayed there must be garlands of flowers around him, and was particularly fond of Hampton Court Palace because here the blue anemones blew wildly in the spring, and later in the year the lilies-of-the-valley perfumed the whole of the house with its crooked chimneys, with the sweetness of their perfume.

The new King frequently played at the Dower Palace, and Nurse Penn came with him. She never let her charge get out of her sight for very long, and only when his masters and tutors insisted on it, would she allow him to visit the schoolrooms with them alone.

He had the best instructors of the day, and under the new régime more men with him than women as was better for him. He did not care for men as much as women, said so, and, most of all, he adored Jane. It was a glorious day with summer a'coming in that Jane spoke of her personal feelings to him. They were playing in the tiny copse, at the end of the garden and sat down to talk.

'I sometimes have a great fear of my future,'

she told him.

'But why should you have fear? I have promised you that I will be a good King, you will do whatsoever you wish to do, and I *will* guard you with my own life.'

'But will they permit Your Grace to be the King?' she asked, a trifle nervously.

'How can they prevent it? I am the only son. What other prince is there?'

'I am always afraid of Mary, the eldest of us all. She has the Church of Rome behind her, and they would do anything to get her back on the throne.'

'But the crown goes to male heirs first, she will have to wait for my death,' and he laughed. Today an apple blossom and Woodruff day, the adult years seemed to be far away and almost matterless. He was looking well, with colour in his cheeks, and that brightness in his eyes which made them look like wild flowers.

She said, 'I always have this fear!'

'But what are you afraid of?'

'I am afraid of death,' she said slowly.

'But who is going to die?'

She stared at him reproachfully, and then suddenly she admitted a truth, which she had weighed out for herself. She said, 'I do not know why I should think this, but I feel that one day Mary will kill me! We both are heirs to the throne.'

'Yes, but there is Elizabeth also. I would

include Elizabeth in the story.'

'Only I feel that she does not come into this story. I see great changes, they have always been with me. I see four women standing here to be queens, and two of them die! They die the hard way,' she made a desperate little movement with her hands, which illustrated what she meant. He saw it, and was horrified!

'You can't mean that?' he asked.

'I do, indeed. I see that the Tudors will come and go, and leave a mark on the world which generations of kings and queens can never obliterate. I am *sure* of that!'

'But I can hear life calling to you now. We shall marry, my sweet, and you will be a fair lady, and a good queen. You will have sons, *my* sons. I am sure of this.'

'Are you sure?'

'So very, very, sure.' He looked well this afternoon, a brightly-coloured boy, with good health in his cheeks, and the same blue eyes that his father had had. His face was more aquiline than his father's had ever been, his hair a soft pale gold, and he had his mother's eyes, kindly tender.

'I always have the fear that I shall die young,' she said tenderly, 'none of us have more than a few years in which to live, and in these hard times when there is so much that is wretched, and men die for their faith, or at the hands of fellow men, then it is harder still!'

He smiled at her.

'I will be a good king,' he promised, 'once I rid myself of my tutors and mentors, then all will be well. Mary will not stand a chance, for I shall make sufficient entry in my will giving the order that neither sisters Mary, nor Elizabeth, succeed me, but that my cousin Jane steps after me to the throne of England! My crown comes in turn, to you, dear Jane, and I do promise you this.'

She blushed rosily, hardly able to believe what she heard and then she said, 'That must not be, for I have no right. Your father left three children of his marriage: the son reigns first, and after that your elder sister, and then Elizabeth! That is the law of the country and only in that order, will they be accepted.'

He shook his head. 'No, that would not be right. Mary is cruel, we all know that! If she comes to the coronation chair, then the streets will be red with blood that she has shed, and I will not allow this. The country knows that she is cruel, and they would not want her as their Queen.'

'But,' and Jane spoke convincingly enough, 'the country knows that she is the rightful queen, and none can discard her when she has the right of birth. She has suffered too much, poor thing, watching *her* good mother die, and that has soured her! She is a staunch Catholic, one cannot blame her for being that, seeing that

Catholicism was the faith of the entire country until your father sought to change it.'

He shook his head.

'I will not allow Mary to be the next queen.'

'But you know that she is the heir apparent, and after her, Elizabeth, and then perhaps myself.'

He flung back his head and laughed gaily at the idea, then tossed his be-feathered velvet cap to the sky, and laughed, as he caught it. 'We shall wed, you and I, when the hour comes, and have a babe, which will be the heir, boy or girl, that does not matter, for either sex can reign after us,' and he laughed again. He infected her with his youthful joyousness, and for a moment she felt that he was right, and that one day he would be a very happy king and she his queen. She took his hand.

'You are very good to me, Edward.'

'I will be your lover, and when the hour comes, I will promise to give you happiness! What is more, we will make this sweet country happy, releasing it from the horrors of bloody Tyburn, from the headsman's axe, and the gallows! We will make neighbour love neighbour, and our sons will reign after us! Not to kill the people they command, but to love them, and teach them to love each other, to the end of their lives.'

'I pray so,' she said.

Whilst they played together, or talked to one

another in the complacent calm of the hayloft they were happy! There was the sweetly musty scent of hay stacked in the far corner; now its greenness had faded to grey, but the lovely scent still clung to it. The palace was ever calm, for the Dowager Queen was herself busy with something which to her looked to be fast becoming the happiest friendship of her life.

There had been a considerable change amongst the men who surrounded her. Norfolk had been cast into prison and his son was now dead. Gardiner, who had suddenly found success fleeing from him and disgrace catching up with him when Kathryn Howard behaved so badly, had retired into his shell, Wriothesley was Chancellor.

But the Seymours were undoubtedly in power, and they meant to make the most of it. Their urge was to seal, sign and deliver, their tie with the throne. Now it mattered nothing that the sister (who had given England a Prince of Wales) had died in the act; the hour would come when her son would reign, and that *would* be their hour!

The boy was crowned on the 28th of February after his father's death, and the night before he spent the time as was the rule sleeping in the palace side of The Tower of London. The Tower had two fulfilments, a palace and a prison, here kings had come for crowning, but here queens, poor women, had come for sentence of death. Anne for one, poor Kathryn for another.

The boy enjoyed himself there, liking the sweet smell of fresh straw on the floor, and the fact that he had been received so nobly and so well, when he rode through the city to the palace this night before his own crowning. In truth London had rejoiced at being rid of the savage old King, who had been so merciless to many, and even more so towards the end of his reign. No woman was safe from his insistent advances. He had, some said, introduced the mode of red hair into the country, so widely that, wherever he had stayed for a single night, some child bore this testament to his triumph.

The Sixth Edward wore white velvet, trimmed with silver, and crystal, and rode to the Abbey Church. His father had done the same thing before him, but he had worn red ruby velvet, and ermine.

The boy waved a plumed hat to the crowd, but he was pale, and had his mother's eyes.

'White means innocence,' some said.

'He comes out of a nice nest,' said some.

It was a magnificent coronation, as the wicked uncles had planned, for now they called the music to which England marched. His uncles hung round him. Somerset bore the crown itself, and it was Cranmer who set it on the lad's head; he must have been only too grateful to think that those devastating years of horror were over, when he wondered how he had ever kept his head on his shoulders.

Now here was a new king.

But those who wanted to establish young Edward realized that the boy would be easy to work with. He was a good kind lad, much like his mother in disposition, though extraordinarily clever when it came to his lesson books. Edward had the inspiration, they all knew.

Cranmer was the one who received the King now, and what his uncles had not recognized was that he was an obstinate boy. He was not going to knuckle under to attack, like his father, he would prefer to fight.

He would stick to the new prayer book, as he had vowed to his father; he would do away with beheadings and burnings, for how he had hated them. This boy desired to have a reign of *peace*. But it was the power behind the King which was the one to be reckoned with. The boy had charm, he was gentle and amiable as his mother had been. Never rude, not commanding, even if he did not always agree with those who would direct him. He had been a brilliant success at his coronation, and his presentation to his people had brought wild cheering! By the autumn it seemed that the whole place had sunk down into far calmer conditions. The new king was popular.

Now it was poor Queen Katherine who was

destined to do the wrong things one after another. There is no doubt that her third widowhood had been a tremendous relief to her. Her third marriage could not have been a happy one, for, when enraged, the King roared at her like a bull and even when he was actually dying that tyrannic strength never seemed to leave him.

Seymour was in charge of the palace at Chelsea, and he had most royal aspirations. The child Jane was now permanently with the Queen Dowager.

They were devoted each to the other, and it is possible that Jane was the first person who knew of Katherine's affair, and romance with Seymour. He was young, and good looking. He had great power over women, for many had lost their hearts to him, and when he employed his charm it was well able to win the day for him.

The marriage was held in secret and even little Jane did not attend it. If she was horrified at the rapidity with which it came about and that it was the Dowager Queen's *fourth* wedding, she said nothing. But very soon after this, she must have become only too well aware of the terrible sequence of events which were closing in around her.

When news of the marriage leaked out it was popular in the city itself. People sympathized with Katherine, but she had been married at sixteen to a decrepit old man, widowed at eighteen, married to another much older man and left widowed and impoverished. Her family despatched her as a lady-in-waiting, with but two dresses to her name. How can I manage? she asked herself.

She did manage, widowed twice, and now not likely to remarry so people thought and then—of all people!—she wedded the King himself. He had been the most tiresome husband in all the world of course, but under it all there had lain love, real love.

Early in her life's sad springtime, she spent most of her time busying herself with ageing husbands, being kindly to gouty legs, and rheumy bad tempers, and helping a man through a life which had become difficult. She slept with him, for not to have slept with one's husband would have been a sin, everybody did it!

Marriage to this old man must have been sickening, but nobody asked. That was considered to be dangerous! No gouty gentleman with a festering sore would have dared look at a jug of water, hot or cold, to bathe in or to drink. One did not do it, and the mode is eternally the mode.

Sometimes, when poor Katie Parr (as some called her) went to the royal bed with the crown over it, and lions and unicorns, there must have been moments when she thought with envy of brave young men, men with muscles and firm skin, men who were good to look upon, and fulfilling in the love vows. But her marriage could not be fulfilled.

She lay there at night, frequently roused to attend to him from time to time. Another dressing was needed. 'God! How that leg hurts me!' he would scream. He had always been a hard master, as she knew, and had filched all the good things from life's happy store cupboard, which made this hour all the harder for him to bear.

He had paid the price for his commitments and his wrongs, but so, alas had his poor Queen!

She suffered badly.

What a contrast it was to be free now, when she came out of the evil-smelling room where the dead King lay, and to know that epoch had gone for ever. Edward would look after her and help her, she knew. Her husband had left her the Dower Palace, where she could live with as many servants as she desired, and every possible comfort. She should be proud, of course, but deep down in her heart lay the emotion which had been there ever since she first met Seymour. It was *love*!

Seymour was master of his future! His family were coming up, the King had adored Jane Seymour, and had been good to the family. He had granted their wishes. Now as Master of the Dowager Queen's household, the Dower Palace, he could get what he wanted from life. And what *did* he want?

* * *

Seymour sought success, and to supplement his association with the crown and now he had an eye on the King's sister Elizabeth. A tomboy, she rode well, a stringy-looking girl, with pale, red hair, and light blue eyes which had no lashes to give them kind shadows. She ran well, had she been a man she would have fought well, he knew.

Master of the Dower Palace, he kept an eye on this princess. The Dowager Queen had the children with her, even Princess Mary, who loved her stepmother, though she hated the dead Anne Boleyn.

Later she changed, when there was a head wanted for the crown, and she saw a fighting foe in the young Elizabeth, who would succeed her. Now she had changed quite a lot, knowing full well that Elizabeth was strong, Perhaps Mary was the first person to realize the defiance, and the fighting spirit of this girl who later in life, was to say, 'I have the body of a woman, but...' and that was the answer. She *had* the male spirit.

'I do not trust my sister,' said Mary, coldly.

'Elizabeth is a good girl,' her stepmother told her, 'a romp, but she will grow out of it later.'

Elizabeth did not trust Mary, and

undoubtedly she guessed that one day she might be at Mary's mercy. And, if so, she would, in all probability, *die*! Queen Mary, as she became, did not keep enemies living an hour longer than she could help.

But Katherine was happy in her new palace! The grounds were delicious, and she had the children with her. The little King visited her formally once in every week, and told her with truth that 'he loved her more than any other woman in the world.'

'And I love you, dear Edward,' she said.

'Always stay in this world to guide me,' he begged.

'As long as God permits. It is God who decides, that does not rest with me.'

He turned, and kissed her. 'You are an angel!' he told her, 'and I want you to stay with me for ever.'

'I will never willingly leave you, Sire,' and she kissed him.

Meanwhile, Seymour was looking about him.

He might be master of the Queen Dowager's household and doing well in this rôle, but he wanted more. Privately, he had consulted those doctors whose appointments made them responsible for the life of the little king. Edward had been a delicate toddler, but the marvellous attention of his amiable old nurse had brought him through. At the same time those responsible were not quite sure that he would live many years. He was very strong at eleven years old, better than he had ever been before, and with an able brain for he was one of our cleverest Kings.

He and the Dowager Queen were immense friends.

She was happy in her new position; she could wander out amongst her flowers without attendant ladies and she could play childish games with the children, but there was of course the one disturbing influence.

This was Tom Seymour, master of her household.

He sought improvement in his position, and he meant to make this advantageously. Mary was an impossible bride, besides a vehement Catholic, hideously ugly, and a vile temper. He ruled her out, but foxy Elizabeth had charm. She was clever, and if annoyed, hit back and hard. She was also gay. But she would have nothing to do with him.

Elizabeth had always had the remarkable gift of being able to put a price ticket on everything in this world, more particularly perchance, a man's love! It was at her own request that she went to Hatfield, where she said that she could study more assiduously (the girl was a bookworm) and so she went.

She would be a great queen if ever she got the chance, so they said, but how would she ever get the chance?

Seymour looked to the Queen Mother herself! He was aware that he attracted her, and she was not clever enough to conceal her admiration, and affection for him. He touched her hand, and she did not rebuke him, as she should have done. There came the pleasant twilight of an April evening, when they walked in the palace gardens together, side by side as equals, and he not the usual foot behind her, as usually was expected of him.

'April is the loveliest month,' she told him.

'May more beautiful. I adore the festivities, and the Queens of May,' and then, acting on a sudden intuition, 'you should be the Queen of the May, Madam!'

She coloured rosily. 'No married lady can be that,' she said.

He risked the chance. Drawing a bow at a venture had always been lucky to him. 'I would have said you were wholly suitable,' he answered and their eyes met.

Falteringly she asked herself could it be that he knew that she had never been wived? Could it be that, even now, well advanced into the distant twenties, and approaching the thirties, she was still unwed, save in name!

She faltered, 'That is not true. . . .'

But he knew that it *had* been true. One of those fortunate guesses which bring a man back to earth, he said. 'I have always admired you, Madam, and I do remember. . . .'

She whispered, 'I am glad,' for now she was feeling giddy with his compliments, and flushed with satisfaction from his promises.

'The greatest lovers are those who love from afar,' he whispered.

She knew that she should not listen. This was madness! She knew that she could forbid him to walk on such dangerous ground, but his be-ringed hand was on her own, and she winced.

'We—we are being foolish,' she said, and weakly, for this took her nowhere at all.

He was kindly. He stopped beside a garden bed, where the blue scillas were withering, the snowdrops dead, but the primroses riotous. He picked a little bunch of them, and laid them in her hand. 'They have the sweetest scent, Madam,' he said.

She took them, and as she did so, their eyes met. She spoke quickly, and without thinking.

'This madness,' she said quickly, 'you forget our two positions, and I owe a duty to my late husband, the King.'

'I stand rebuked, Madam,' and he said it so sorrowfully that instantly she relented.

'You did no wrong. We are old friends.'

'I would we were eternal friends.'

Joyously she said, 'That can be, and it shall be. I will be yours and you will be mine for ever. Friends who can talk of old times!'

That night she could not sleep, for she thought only of him. Had she been wrong to encourage him, but right to keep him in his place? Next morning, when her maid brought the special breakfast to her, there was a bowl of primroses set on it for her, and, when she asked whence it had come (suspecting Princess Elizabeth, or little Lady Jane Grey), the maid blushed, and said it had been Seymour.

As she ate her breakfast, she knew that all this was wrong. Later in the day she would speak to him, but she never did. Maybe she was in love herself, deeply so. Maybe she had already committed herself too far, but she knew that she was truly happy for the first time in her whole life; she knew that she wanted this man more than any other man in the world.

'It must never happen again,' she warned him, when the opportunity made itself clear.

'I stand corrected,' he told her.

But more flowers came.

The affair raced ahead, and she knew that it thrilled her. None of her husbands had ever done this for her before, and she had not been able to believe that it was true. It was a wet spring day, coming towards evening, and the dripping world still made its own music. The two of them were alone when he spoke to her.

'I have known you so long, and have always loved you. If you were an ordinary girl, and you *are* a girl, though thrice wived, and if I were an ordinary man, then I should say right here and now, marry me? Anywhere, any time, and as you will. . . .'

'We must not speak of such things.'

'Love talks this way, and I believe that we have always loved one another,' he said.

She could not deny it.

Now she saw three husbands, all much older men, receding into the past, and she thanked the powers-that-be that, this time, it would be a young man of her own age. He had youth, and the flashing eyes, rich with promises; he could say things to her with those enchanting eyes of his, which he dare not say with his lips, for he still remembered that she *was* a queen, and could, if she wished, have him beheaded.

After a moment he whispered, 'It could be a secret marriage. Our own secret.'

There is no girl to whom this does not have some appeal, 'I dare not,' she said.

'I will give you courage.'

'This is not lack of courage, but I owe a duty to my position and to the children.'

'The children that you will bear, *our* children,' he reminded her and that won her.

Privately she arranged a trousseau. It was of course, true that she had wasted very little time, for her husband had died in late January, and this was only June. But Seymour was an old love. Lord Seymour of Sudeley, would give her happiness she knew, and she had ever cared for him, and the whole thing was secret as it had to be!

The very plan for it infected her with a childish delight. They would meet surreptitiously in a small church, which he knew well, and the friars could keep a secret. She entered it for the first time in her life, on a night at six o'clock, and they were married with the daylight fast dying, for as yet it was not summer, and walked out each going their separate ways from the door. But that night he came to her when she was supping, something he frequently did, so that there was nothing new to attract local interest in it. They talked after the meal had gone, and the golden flagons of wine were on the table.

He touched her with licentious fingers!

'Oh, not this, my lord,' she begged him, 'not yet.'

'Surely my own wife does not refuse me?' he demanded and she blushing still, knew that he was right.

When eventually she fell asleep it was to dream, that this had been the happiest day of all her life. She was a wife. Not maid, nor widow, but his wife, and none knew.

Little did she realize that page boys had had an eye to the keyhole, and the younger maids of honour (ever ready for a delicious piece of scandal) had giggled together, and that, before many months had passed by, she would find herself with child by him. For tonight she was his wife, his love, widowed three times but never wived before, and the whole arrangement sounded to be like a fairy tale.

'I am so happy,' she whispered to him.

'You shall be happy for ever,' he promised her.

FIVE

> We look before and after;
> We pine for what is not;
> Our sincerest laughter
> With some pain is fraught;
> Our sweetest songs are those that tell
> Of saddest thought.
>
> *Shelley*

DURING that summer Katherine was completely happy in the Dower Palace. The gardens were so exceptionally beautiful, and the child Jane was ever with her. The summer of 1548 was, one might say, a happy one with good weather, no insurgent heat, save at the start, and there had been fewer alarms about plague being in the air. Maybe it was heat which produced the plague, some argued?

At last the newly-wived Queen Katherine discovered for the first time that she was pregnant. The morning sickness assailed her and so vigorously that she guessed others would be suspicious. She admitted the truth, far better that, than for a scandal to arise.

It had all happened too quickly of course, and she soon lost the admiration and the love which she had always experienced from a country which had been ready to welcome her as a sixth wife, and grateful for all that she had done as the Queen of Henry the Eighth.

'I married him secretly,' she told Jane.

'I would have wished to have been with you.'

'Yes, yes, I know, but I thought it was our secret. His and mine! We were so happy, and I am so overjoyed over the baby. So glad.'

'I will stay with you?' the girl asked.

'You shall stay for as long as ever you wish,' was the answer, 'you shall be the elder daughter to this new little brother or sister. I love you, Jane dear, I always have done, and I always shall.'

They embraced one another, these two, who were perhaps closer to the affectionate bond of mother and daughter, than to any other in this world. They held hands. It was Jane who started sewing for the babe, little garments of which the child would have far too many, and which were elaborately embroidered with the initials on them.

It was a lazy summer. The King visited the Dower Palace once every week, and they walked in the gardens. He did not like Seymour, and made his dislike felt, so that his visits always came when Seymour himself was elsewhere. The man must have become aware of the fact that he was unpopular, surely?

Katherine was wildly happy!

She had a kind message from the Princess Mary, who adored children herself, and another from Hatfield House, where the young Elizabeth was staying with her mentors and tutors. The first time that Katherine saw the leaves yellowing in the garden she told herself, 'My hour—my greatest hour must be at hand,' and rejoiced.

Jane was goodness itself and never left her. Her own people seemed satisfied that she should do this, though after a time they wrote asking her to return home, but she refused to leave when the Queen was ill, and would stay until the confinement was over.

Princess Elizabeth was in the house, and just as the ex-Queen had almost completed her full time, and the birth was imminent, the young Princess quarrelled with Seymour himself! He believed, perchance foolishly, that becoming espoused to the widow of a king, had given him something of a royal connection, even more than he had had, when his sister shared the throne.

The row began one night. Elizabeth was a boisterous, full-blooded girl, and, although she was wretchedly thin, was sturdy, a girl who could challenge any man if she so wished. Seymour gave her an order, which she promptly disobeyed, and he, losing his temper, for he was hot-blooded and tempered too, slapped the Princess for disobeying his orders.

Instantly she turned, and snatching up her own little riding whip laid on the side, and cut his face with it, hitting him quite savagely.

'I am a king's daughter, and a king's sister,' she reminded him between her set teeth, whilst those pale blue lashless eyes of hers, were the colour of steel.

Seymour was dismayed at her arrogance, hurt as well, actually bleeding and trying to stem the flow, but she defied him, all queen, all power and suddenly he knew that he could never hope to conquer her.

Even her stepmother had been angered, and had sent the girl to her room on bread-and-water for two days. But Elizabeth had emerged from this, anything but apologetic. She insisted yet again that as a King's sister, and her father's own daughter, no man had the right to strike her, and that she must have an apology.

That was the last thing that he would have given to her!

'Then I shall return to Hatfield,' the girl said, 'please make the proper arrangements for me.'

Reluctantly, the Queen made these arrangements, and was herself too unwell to see her stepdaughter off. It was Jane who returned to her room from this task and told the Queen what had happened.

'She has gone,' she said.

'Was she saddened in the end?'

'I did not think so; she was very angry, and said that none would ever be happy in this house for it was accursed!'

Poor Katherine tried to cover her own superstitious alarm at this remark. 'That is not true! How could it be true? She is a virago at times, poor child!'

Jane tried to help her.

She said, 'Let us forget that it ever happened. I believe that in life it pays only to remember the sweet and kindly things. They have a rightful place in this hard world, the cruel things should be forgotten, and cast from us,' and the child spoke quietly.

'You are a very dear child.'

The girl touched the older woman. 'My own dear one,' she whispered, 'do not get so agitated.'

'I know. I do know.'

They got on together extremely well, these two, and they always would, but Jane was worried for her adored aunt, as she always called the Queen. One evening, nearer still to the hour when the royal babe would be born, she sat there in Katherine's bedroom talking to her.

'You love my lord Seymour, very dearly, do you not?' was what she asked.

'Very, very much.' The eyes of the Queen were weary now, for the child was large and heavy, and she, coming so close to her hour, grew afraid for it. 'He is so good to me!'

The girl who was watching her, said very gently, 'I have fears that my Lord Seymour would rather wed the crown itself, than woo the woman who wore it.'

'But that is a very cruel thing to say!' and the poor Queen was startled by it. 'He is a very dear man, my love, my own love,' and then, for her heart was filled with abject dismay, 'I would have you love him as I do.'

'I love him as I admit, he has great beauty, and is a fine figure of a man, beautifully made but somehow there is something about him which amazes and disturbs me.'

'You do not trust him?' It so alarmed the poor Queen that the girl could say this, that she almost wept. 'He is good to every woman whom he meets, and so gentle.' Then she added, 'He much wished to wed your cousin Elizabeth.'

'But she would not take him?'

After a moment, in which the poor Queen was dismayed that the girl could be so near the truth, she said, 'She would not have him, for Elizabeth is a perverse girl. The Queen makes up her own mind in her own way. The Spanish Prince would be good to her.'

'But surely she would not have him?'

'They do say...' and then she dropped her eyes. It would be unwise to talk too much, and then have something undesirable happen.

Jane spoke again. Her own education had been remarkable for a girl of that period, and she had worked hard at her lessons. Perhaps she wanted much of the sweetness of her own life, and was trying to understand what it offered to her. Young Edward had always told her, 'When I die, I have left you the throne of England, because you are the best of the four women who stand in line for it! But I have left the throne itself to you, my coz., because you are wise. Mary would turn the country back to the Catholic faith and destroy too many. I know that Elizabeth would keep it as it is, but can be a difficult girl.'

Jane spoke eagerly. 'I do not think that it is wise that the Queen-to-be should come from some other land?'

'No, that should not be.'

'As the French Queen, Mary of Scotland.'

'I know. I believe that the Prince of Spain is already negotiating for the hand of Princess Mary, a strange girl, and difficult to help, for she has a cruel streak in her, and strikes me as being the friend of death.'

'I pray not.'

The woman, who had herself been a queen, perhaps in the most difficult time of all Henry's wives, said, 'I knew that from the first time that I saw her Mary would cause suffering. I have never understood her, but does anyone? Yet, when he lay dying she did all that she could to help him and all of us. She actually fought to save his life.'

'And then he died.'

'Yes, he died. Life comes to an end for all of us. The bell rings, and we recognize the call and respond to it. We get up and we go for ever maybe.'

The girl changed the subject and spoke of the future. 'They do say that the young Spanish Prince is visiting England to wed the Princess Mary. Would it be wise, think you? He is a Catholic which she would love, but could he not harm England?'

The woman who had been the last of Henry's six queens, shook her head. 'I do not think that I would want Spain to return to England, for under everything she is embittered, and changed. She frets for ever for her poor mother. I would not want Spanish children to inherit the throne, which is Edward's now. I would not like that.'

The child was disturbed.

She trembled for the future, and the Queen Mother also. She was nearing the hour of her own delivery; it is an hour which most women dread, for it is fraught with suffering, bringing a new life into the world. The child could come within the week. The wise thing to do was to wait for life to make its decisions, and not try to force anything now, at this moment. Once the baby came it would be easier to decide what to do next, where to go, or if to stay. The girl rose.

'I will not keep you talking for it will only tire you, and you need to rest now, and keep all strength to bring into the world another life.'

The woman, who had been a Queen Consort herself, smiled kindly. 'I am not tired, my dear, and am quite ready to sit up talking to you for you make me very happy! I wonder what name we shall give this boy? I feel that he will be a boy, I hope so! I seek a name for him, hope for him, and joy for all of us.'

She sounded sad. In these last few days she had been told by one of the wise women, who nursed mothers and babes, that it always appeared to become more difficult. Once the delivery began, then it was easier. It was waiting for it which was such a torment.

The girl slipped away to bed, and during that very night, Queen Katherine, widow of the eighth Henry, and his last wife (now married to the man whom she truly loved) was taken ill! She felt the first pain come quivering through her, like a knife thrust deeply, galvanized herself, to face it, to close with it, and to win.

She knew that it had been Seymour himself who had urged the secret marriage; she herself would have waited longer to the memory of the man, who had married her, making her wife and queen in one! But Seymour was anxious to establish himself in closer bondage with the royal family. He was a man of aspirations, for wealth, and for power, and all these he believed he could get now by availing himself of the fact that his cousin was the King of England and, through their relationship he could get everything! He knew how fond the boy was of his stepmother, and realized that this was a wise step to take.

It was quite true that the poor widowed Queen had never thought of this man's avarice for high position, for riches, and for everything that a clever marriage could bring to him. Although Katherine looked far older than she was (still in the twenties) this had come because her marriages had been such hard work. Any woman who survived Henry the Eighth as a husband, must have been strong, but considerably weakened by the experience.

Now, with all that behind her, poor Katherine knew that she was avid for romance. Seymour could give it to her. She admired his good looks; he had the bluest dark eyes, which could sparkle with the sheer joy of living! Her own eyes were gypsy dark; she had always been a very dark woman, and it was said that this darkness was the quality that the royal King Hal had killed for women. Had not poor Anne Boleyn been dark as a raven, with eyes like ripe blackberries in an autumn hedgerow.

They had met when she had gone as a lady-in-waiting to the court then at Greenwich Palace, soon after, her second husband had died, and was wretchedly poor. Ladies-in-waiting were fed and housed, and occasionally amiably spoilt, she had been told. She had got very little out of it, but the food here was good. She would save and get herself some better clothes, which she most needed.

But, on this, the first day that they had ever met, he had called to her to come nearer and to speak with him. That had been at Greenwich Palace also, on one of those vivid March mornings, with the bright promise of spring sunshine and blue anemones in the flower beds, and the little Lent lilies waving in the wind.

She had approached him with fear in her heart. He had been king, he had told her that she had dark eyes, and all his life they had attracted him!

Half of her was encouraged; he was so kind. The other half afraid that he would be angered with her, and then have her head chopped off! The story of the death of Kathryn Howard was still recent news.

After that meeting he had constantly sent for her; when she came, he demanded aid from her, and so had discovered that she was good at nursing, and persuaded her to help with his bad leg.

When he asked her to marry him, she could not say 'no' to him. *That* would have meant death, she was sure of it! She would ever forget how she had trembled on her bridal day, married hurriedly, in the little chapel attached to the palace at Greenwich. She remembered the sweet scent of lilies, the sound of young boys singing, and her own apprehensions, half of terror and dismay, half of joy that she would be a Queen (the first lady in England), wife of the King himself.

There had been no marriage night, which perhaps she had dreaded most of all, for, although she had been wedded twice before, she had never yet been a wife! It seemed that Henry had never thought of anything of that kind! Indeed, how much the man had aged! she told herself.

Marriage had been very much like the old times, and she had slept night after night in that room with the horrible stench of that suppurating leg of his, the curious noises he made in his sleep, the groans, the snores, and the dismay that the pain could be so cruel. He would lie there muttering to himself, and knowing that although he was yet again a bridegroom, it meant nothing to him, nothing at all, for now he had come to the end of the road and had little longer to live!

But this was different!

Now the man who sought her hand in marriage was tall and slender. He had no abutting flabby stomach, or fat legs, and he did not waddle when he walked! Seymour was good-looking; he was well used to women and everything that they desired of him, and they would always find him to be a generous lover. He walked quickly, in sharp strides, and she watched him going through the Knot Garden surprised at the sheer beauty of him and the self pride which made him so erect, so proud and oh, so strong.

At first she thought that he had come to the Dower Palace to visit her, because he was one of the king's relatives and needed consolation and amiable attention. It was quite some time before she discovered that Seymour was searching for a wife, and when it came to choice he was fastidious. All the Seymours wanted everything, though poor Jane (who had been the King's wife) had been the very opposite of this. Tom Seymour was searching for some girl of good birth, and education, so that she fitted into his dream of a fine house to live in, hostess at attractive parties, the power to make him greater still and achieve all his wildest dreams.

When he thought of the princesses, he had never for a moment looked as high as a *queen*, but now, this was exactly what he *was* doing!

She liked him he knew. She was weak in many ways, over modest, and neither of these were his personal faults. She had realized that he had royal desire, for there had been a time when those handsome eyes of his were on the Princess Elizabeth herself and then he had declared that her temper was too virulent, no man could ever be truly happy with a little virago, such as she was!

Maybe that was half-true. Elizabeth was bad tempered when she made up her mind, and she *did* want her own way. What was even more, she got it!

'But she is a good girl,' her stepmother had told him, and insistently.

He laughed at the bare idea of that. 'Is marriage the arrangement to keep good girls good girls?' he asked and laughed because she was shocked at the idea. She was not used to men, he knew. She would never understand the laxity of the young ladies in the Maids' Dormitories, and the naughty behaviour of gay young courtiers who squirmed away into the dormitories behind the big tapestries which covered men, the walls, and were sometimes found a'bed with a fair damsel!

There was no doubt about it that Katherine Parr was pure. When he asked her to marry him, she could not believe that it was true.

'I have been married three times a'ready, Sir,' she said quietly. 'I was wedded the first time when I was but sixteen years of age.'

He warmed to her then.

'Ours would not be the marriage of arrangement, but of the heart itself, and that is how the best marriages are made. I do promise you that ours would be the bond of love.'

She told herself that she did not love him.

How could she marry again so soon, when it was but January when her third husband had died, and this was the month of roses? He made her take a glance at her reflection and see how young she still looked. As yet she had few lines, and had kept some of the exquisite colour she had had as a girl. Their marriage would be the first real marriage that she had had, for he had extorted from her the story of the first husband, who had been dying when she married him, and the second one also old for her, and not madly in love. Of her marriage to the King who had already had sufficient of love and marriage, and had chosen her, but to give him a son, not to satisfy a carnal appetite, but to comfort him in his sickness. To bind up his aching leg with fresh bandages, and to console him through the days when he trod the path which leads to that dark valley from which there is no return.

He urged that they married soon.

Summer was here, and he would not be responsible for his behaviour if she tried him too hard. He had been spurred on when the child Elizabeth had cut him with that riding whip of hers, and he had promised himself that one of these days he would give her the surprise of her life, and that he would pay her back for that cut! In plenty, he told himself, *indeed* in plenty!

To marry her stepmother, put him into a position which associated itself with fatherhood. He grinned at the thought.

'Why should we wait?' he asked the lady, when they walked in the gardens with the stars breaking through the night sky, and the sweet scent of lilies-of-the-valley everywhere.

'My husband has not been dead six months as yet. It would be bad behaviour to remarry too soon.'

He said—and truthfully—'He was never your husband, and you have told me so! If you had never told me of it, I still should have known, for the years make men impotent. It is the last gift which nature plucks from them, then laughs to see how sad they become.'

She had tried to argue with him for the sake of Henry, who, in her own way, she *had* loved. It had never been true marriage as she knew, and perhaps the most shocking thing was that although she had been wedded three times already, not one of those times had been true marriage, and she was still a virgin.

She told him so.

He laughed when she told him, slapping his slender thigh with amusement, and the dark eyes radiantly beautiful.

'When I wed you, my own sweet lady,' he said, 'do not expect that there will be no fee to pay, nothing that I shall not ask of you! I may have been a'bed with a virgin, but when I rose from that bed, she was a virgin no more! I marry you, because I ask you to be my wife. My own dear wife.'

She knew then that she could not deny him! She would marry him, and as soon as he wished it. She said so.

SIX

> He wears the rose of youth
> Upon him.
> *William Shakespeare*

IT WAS June when they were quietly married.

None knew of the ceremony about to take place, save the witnesses, two countrymen brought to the village for the occasion, from one of the bridegroom's estates, and pledged to secrecy. The bride did not even know their names.

Yet the mystery was convincing and exciting to her. It took place at night, and they entered the dark little church, with the flicker of bright candles, and when she saw her youthful bridegroom waiting for her, her heart turned over with joy! This, she told herself, is the moment of my life! A bride at sixteen, widowed at seventeen, a bride again (and yet once more widowed) the third time a queen, and now the wife of the man she truly loved.

To her it was the most exciting ceremony of all her life, even if her view of it was smudged by her own happy tears. I love him with all my heart and soul, she told herself. God is indeed good to me. God has given me all that a woman could want. A brave young husband, and later children to bless us.

For she had ever adored children.

They finished the ceremony, and returned to the Dower Palace to sup, arriving there as though he were still a visiting friend come to share a meal with her, a dear friend, of course, but certainly not her bridegroom of this very day. The palace became hushed, the feast had gone. It was not unusual for the two of them to sit on talking.

My night, the happiest night of all my life, she told herself, the girl who had had three previous marriages, yet never had felt the thrill of real love, and the depths of this ravishing emotion. He stayed and held her in his arms.

'I love you for ever,' he told her.

'I pray that you outlive me. I could not bear to lose yet another husband. Life has been too terrible. My youthfulness consorting with old age, with pain and suffering, and with death.' Again she thought of how she had knelt beside Henry until his last breath came.

'I will outlive you,' he promised, and he kept that vow! He was not a tender man; he did not love deeply, and although she did not suspect this, the hour would come when he was sick of his ex-Queen, and had found it brought him little. That he would seek to be rid of her, for his eye would have turned back to the failing health of the young King, and to the red-headed command of the Princess Elizabeth, who one day—he was convinced of this—would herself be queen regnant!

Seymour planned for the future.

He left, of course, before the dawn touched the sky with pearl. He slipped from the window, and out into the night, across the fields which lay behind the Dower Palace, to the house further up the Thames reach where he lived alone. He whistled as he went, laughed to himself, an ambitious man in love with life, and boasting that he would get more from it than many of his contemporaries. What a secret he held. The Queen's husband! This is living life, he told himself.

And she, still sleeping the fond sleep of satisfaction, turned in her bed and dreamt again the sweetness of his touch, and the tender whisperings he had left with her, and her own irrepressible happiness.

They had kept their secret for some months until the moment came when she could not withhold the truth longer. It was the way that they had planned. As yet none knew of it. Little Jane recognized the fact that they were fast friends and appreciated this. She herself was half-afraid of Seymour for he could be commanding, and was not a good Churchman which she was. But he *was* the Queen's friend, and she desired above all other things that the dear kind Queen should be happy.

When that hot summer reached its meridian, and the longest day had come to die again, and the tawny flowers came into the garden beds to replace the sweet roses and lilies of summer time, everything changed. The day that the Queen walked in the garden and noticed that the rowan tree was thick with vivid red berries, she recognized the truth within herself.

To the outside world she had been known through these months as Katherine, the Queen, but now, what would she be? She was sure that the young King would be kind to her, for he loved her, and would give her everything that he could. But he was having trouble dealing with the stern demands of his mother's people.

She told the King first, and he was kind to her. But the news slipped out, and the city greeted it with loud guffaws.

So this was the lady who had always posed as being so virtuous, and so good! Married four times, and three of them to men old enough to be her father, had they wished to be. Each of them had left her widowed and alone. The last time she had followed the King himself to Windsor to lay him beside the Queen he declared to have loved best, the one who had borne him a son, King Edward the Sixth, his own Queen Jane. Then the world had been sorry for her, and had admired the way that she had tended him, and Henry the Eighth was a vicious invalid, never pausing to be pleasant about his malady, but to rate at those who tended him. Then within a few months of his death she married the man whom she now said she had loved all her life.

Seymour laughed about the gossip, though he could not have been too pleased, really! Jane herself was wretched that they should say cruel things about the woman she knew was so kind, and who had been so good to her. But this is a fickle world. She little knew, poor child, how true she would find this to be.

Already Seymour himself was finding difficulties in his marriage, and he was a proud man. The crown had come close to him, but never close enough. He realized that he should have insisted that the young Elizabeth would espouse him. The woman he had married was now no longer a queen; nor was she even the mother of the king, for her marriage had never been more than a name, and she had had no child. In fact, she had been a virgin when he married her.

'Three husbands and still a virgin,' he had said to himself, 'there is something remarkable about that.'

She was not very happy in these months of her pregnancy for she was ill. She suffered from bad headaches, and constant weakness. The person kindest to her was Jane, the child who nursed her with very real affection, and did in truth care deeply for her. Seymour himself seized hold of the chance to enjoy himself at court.

He was a man who went with the younger courtiers to the maids of honours' dormitory, when the aged Duchess (whose duty was to mind the girls and make sure that they stayed as maids), was asleep, and it was possible to slip into the room unnoticed. For although she would not have admitted it for the world, the Duchess was a shade deaf, and slept like a log.

'And that is all to the good,' said one of the more lively maids of honour, 'for she would be reduced to ashes if she knew what goes on at night in the dormitory,' and she had laughed.

None was more willing to share the thrill than Tom Seymour, and he did this.

'My wife is pregnant,' he told the girls.

They teased him. 'And your son will not be a prince. Too difficult! Now had it been the previous husband she could have borne a noble Duke of York, and that *would* have been pleasant!' They understood Seymour far better than he realized.

'My wife is not well with her pregnancy,' he said, 'she is quarrelsome, and irritable. She suffers from distressing headaches, and weeps much. It is no place for me.'

'Forget all that since you cannot help her,' the

girls told him and encouraged a merry presence in their dormitory, where amusement went on until the dawn. He wondered if maybe he had rushed the marriage? He was a vain man, well aware of his own good looks, and his powers, and he was now not sure that his right royal marriage had been unwise.

How did the royal family themselves accept the news?

By now the Princess Mary was keeping herself entirely apart. She feigned to have no interest in what was going on, lived in the country and although she had been amazingly devoted to her step-mother, when her father was alive, now did not worry herself at all. Elizabeth was at Hatfield with the Salisburys, learning wisely. She was an apt pupil, delighted in book learning and dedicated herself so devoutly to lessons that she became thin and pale. It was true that she was living through a magnificent education, but also true that she was weakening her own body by her vigilance, and attention to her books.

The King was amiable.

'I ask a brother of you, Madam,' he told his stepmother, 'if I could make him a Duke of York, I would indeed, but that is beyond my power. Give me a brother?'

'I will do my best, Sire,' she promised.

It was Jane who was the devoted one. Jane who tended her, and cared for her and who comforted her when she wept. She was well aware of the fact that her husband was flirting with the King's sisters. He had gone into the country to visit the Princess Mary, who had received him coldly, though he did find that Elizabeth was more responsive. She was tiring of constant lesson books, and greybeard tutors and masters eternally instilling knowledge within her. He made her ride with him, and that thrilled her. It was heavenly to taste the warm autumnal air again, to ride through the Hertfordshire woods, and to drink in the pleasantness of morning mist, and hot midday sun.

If I had waited longer, he thought, it could have been the princess, and not the dull widowed queen, and he reproached himself.

Jane thought only of Katherine.

'Today is the first of August,' she told her, 'and 'ere this month is out, you should be holding a boy babe in your arms.'

'You are good to me, my dear child,' said the unhappy woman, and then, 'where is my husband?'

'At Hatfield.'

'With Elizabeth?'

The girl invented a story, if only to make her happier. He had gone there on some message of importance, sent thither by those who were guardians of the young King.

'He will persuade her,' she said, and with

pride.

'Elizabeth is hard to talk round,' Jane told her.

'But he has ways with him!'

'Yes,' said the young girl, and with some doubt, for these 'ways' of her kinsman had frequently agitated her.

Katherine was taken ill a fortnight before her time, and in the night. At first the murmur of small pains within her did not distress her unduly; she had no wish to call the nurse, an unqualified woman, who had been installed for some months already in case of accident was living on the fat of the land, and the best out of a bottle, and enjoying every moment of it, so she said. She watched the lazy day draw itself out of the darkness of night, already the hours of daylight were closing in, and morning took longer to dismiss the stars and usher in the sun. The first person who came to her room was, as usual, Jane. She had slept badly. She was a girl who had always had strange emotions, was endowed with something which today one might call 'second sight'.

She had, during this last week, been sure that the child would come before its time, that the birth would be difficult, and that nothing would go right! Not for the world would she have told the dear Queen this, but on this particular morning, she woke long before day was born, and grew so tired of lying there, that she rose, dressed and came to her stepmother's room. She had no intention of awaking her, or of disturbing her in any way but heard her cough, and instantly there had been a tiny groan following it.

She knew the truth.

She opened the door quietly and came into the room.

'It is Jane, Your Grace,' she said, softly.

The Queen heard her, and with relief. In the last hour the pains had managed to become faster, and more acute. She had been wondering if it was not time for her to awaken the old nurse? Now help had come to her.

'You are there, Jane?'

'Yes, Madam,' and she dropped a curtsey, 'you are unwell?'

'I—I think the babe has started on his j—journey.'

'I will call the nurse.'

The Queen called her back. 'Wait a moment! I want a word first. This babe, this small child, I want you to guard him for me, Jane. I am afraid. I do not think somehow that my husband would be a fond father. I see ahead of me, that which is worrying. If . . . if I died. . . .'

'You will not die, Madam. All women feel this when labour begins, but babes come into the world, and live to grow into men with their mother still there, to smile at them.'

The Queen gave a little groan, gripped the

coverlet closer whilst the pain accelerated, and then calmed down again. 'It is worse than I thought possible,' she said.

'I will fetch the nurse, for she can help you.'

'None can help me, Jane dear. This is the burden that all daughters of Eve carry, to bring sons into the world, and suffer for those sons. It—it is worse than they told me.'

'They say, dear Madam, that if the pain comes sharply at first then the bearing time is quicker.' And then seeing that another pain was starting. 'Let me send for the nurse.'

She went to the door. There was the houseling stool against the wall, where night and day the pages sat waiting to run messages, and fulfil their duties. Today the stool was empty. She knew what had happened, the one on duty had slipped down to the big kitchens in the cellars of the palace, to avail himself of food of some kind. She called out sharply, 'Page? Page?'

Because there came no reply, she ran nimbly down the passage way, and called over the stone stairs which led down. This time she got an answer and the boy came up to her, his mouth full of some delicacy which he had filched.

'You had no right to desert your post.'

'I was hungry, your ladyship.'

'Hungry or not, you had no right. Now be quick. The nurse. I want the nurse.'

His eyes grew round with interest. 'Yes, your ladyship.' and he had turned to flee to the cellar where the nurse slept. Through the big kitchens, which smelt of strong smoke, for they were getting the fires up again, after the dull time of night, of food frying, and of hot meat. He woke the woman, lying in a huddle in her clothes, for she never bothered to change them.

'Who is it? who's there ... damn you!' she asked.

'I am the page sent from the Queen to fetch you.'

'The Queen...!' She struggled up, knowing immediately that the hour had come. They still spoke of Katherine as 'The Queen', because Seymour preferred it this way. She turned off the frowsty mattress on the stone floor, and pulled up her stockings which had slipped down her hairy old legs into her shoes. 'Is it day or night? It seems as though light were coming ... what is it ... where am I?'

'It is morning. About seven of the clock.' He giggled a little, knowing she had not got it in her power to punish him. 'You were drunk last night, and pay the price for it today.'

'My head...' and she grabbed the thinning grey hair hanging down in dirty curls. Once it had been golden hair which had attracted young men, she remembered, but time had dealt harshly with her. She was old and ugly now. 'I'll come,' she said.

'Now. Lady Jane demands you come now.'

'Who is the chit that she dare command me?'

and she mouthed hideously coarse oaths.

'The Lady Jane is someone.' He paused, well aware that maybe he said what he should never say. 'Men tell me one day she could be the Queen of England. . . .'

'Never. The King will have sons of his own.'

'They could be her sons, too,' and he giggled, then from the door. 'I was to tell you to hasten. Be quick, or they'll have me whipped. Be quick, and come to her.'

'I'll be coming.'

He went back to the wooden stool where he would sit on duty until the courtyard clock struck nine in the morning, and then he would be relieved of duty, and sent to rest. He ran fast, well aware that great things were happening here. Today a babe would be born, and the babe could easily be a king or queen of England.

When he got back to his post of duty, the doctor was coming to her ladyship. His wig was awry, he hated the world to know that he was bald, but he was. His gown was marked with spots where he had dropped food when dining, and had never troubled to clean the stains. He peered unpleasantly, as though but half-seeing, but then his eyebrows were bushy as a thicket, and the hairs veiled his sight at times. Not for the world would he have had them cut or treated in any way.

The boy listened at the door.

He heard Katherine speaking. 'It is so much

worse than I ever thought it would be, and the times between so short. I cannot bear it.'

'Madam, it always seems worse at first, and then lessens. We will have the charcoal lamp lit, for that will ease it.'

'How long will it be?'

There was a pause, obviously he did not wish to commit himself. Then he said, 'There are medical aids I can give, and will but not yet. When did it start,' and when she said, 'That is but three hours back. Three hours is no time in which a babe is born. No time.'

'I am prepared,' said the Queen, and courageously, then another pain corkscrewed through her, and she groaned.

The doctor and the girl Lady Jane, came out of the room as the nurse went in. The page stood up to order, his eyes quiet, not moving a muscle, and they, worried for the patient, said not a single word to him.

'It seems to be distressing her badly,' Jane said.

'Yes indeed, but let me tell you, the first time that she kisses her son, all memory of this pain will die. She will forgive him every agony he has caused her, and be glad!'

'But now ... now? Is there nothing that we can do to help her?' asked the girl.

The arrival of the nurse helped Katherine somewhat, and they brought the charcoal lamp for her, and the fumes made everyone feel sleepy. Jane spent the morning in and out of the bedroom and already the news had travelled to the gossipy city. There they bet on a son, a boy, who, if things worked out well for him, would possibly get to the throne.

'Not with Princess Mary ready to pounce,' said some, and laughed at the bare idea.

The news went round, then the crowds tired of it for Katherine was no longer queen, and therefore not so interesting. Her husband was a man, thoroughly disliked by the populace for it was said that the Seymours fought for their own ends, not caring who lived or died. If Tom Seymour had a son by the woman who had been Henry's last wife, undoubtedly he would work to edge the boy closer to the Stone of Scone.

'We live in thrilling times,' said the crowd sojourning about the little amiable streets of London. Bread Lane. Milk Alley, and such. When the sun died early, and the mist (which smelt of stagnation) arose thickly from the river, they went inside to drink. The one person who stayed with Katherine was the child, and she never left her.

'I will stay with you for ever,' she had promised.

She was now thirteen years old, and her cousin Lady Anne Seymour was to be wed at Isleworth. There had been much talk of the marriage and Jane was given a very special gown to be worn, for she was one of the bridesmaids.

She thought of it with thrill.

Tom Seymour, who was in gay good humour had dined in state with the family in the great baronial hall there. He had made the Jester foretell the future, and the Jester who had not wished to be dragged into this, had at first hung back, then he had predicted that Tom had married, and the first babe of the marriage would be a son.

'How,' commanded Seymour, when the meal seemed to flag. Two musicians had failed to come and he was in his cups and angry at the poorness of the melodies. He had needed music he said, and forced others to play.

'I give the orders,' he announced.

Older brothers and uncles tolerated him, seeing that he was 'in his cups', and right merry with it.

'I give the orders,' he had said.

So they sang, and played, and far into the night the entertainment went on and Tom Seymour returned home.

Tom Seymour was a strange man and noisy with it. He was sure of himself, wedded to an ex-Queen and now prayed for the babe to be a boy. A son and he saw himself safe for the throne. The present King could not last long, he would not have lasted as long as he had done, had it not been for the wondrous services of his old nurse. And next to him, before any of these girls, *my son*, Seymour told himself.

He sat on drinking and waiting for the news to come. Much later, when he was awakened from a fuddled sleep, he was told that the birth was now imminent, and he rose, unsteadily enough. He laid a firm hand on a pageboy's shoulder, the boy nearly cowed down by his weight, and they went to the confinement room.

He wished that he were not quite so drunk, but what man is there who is not entitled to get a little drunk on the day when his heir is born? He tried to quicken his step on the flagged flooring of the great hall, and almost slipped, having to jerk himself up again.

He smelt the deadening stench of the charcoal burner as he entered the stuffy room itself; no window had ever been opened within it for the last few weeks, lest the Queen caught a cold through it. He heard the spluttering noisily infuriated crying of the very newly-born, and he saw that little Jane Grey was coming towards him with a bundle in her arms. 'Pretty girl!' was what he thought.

The women were busily occupied with his wife, and it was one who brought the babe to him.

'My son?' he said.

'It is a daughter.'

He stared, unable to follow what she said, looked, and squirmed a little. 'Not a girl! My God! Never a daughter.' And then in a rush of fury, 'This country is too full of girls, and every one of them thinks that she had a right to the throne of England. That ugly Mary with her prayings and her penances, her fasting days, and all the rest of it. Young Elizabeth, we have sufficient daughters.'

'She is a very beautiful girl,' said Jane gently.

She was trying to soothe the weak crying of the babe and he, half drunk, but sobering with the news, stared down at the babe which she held in her arms.

He stared at the babe.

She was like her mother, with thick dark hair, that silky supple hair of the newly-born, and he was sure that her eyes would match it. A *girl*, he thought. He had laughed at the royal master who had been cursed with daughters, or stillborn infants of the right sex, but with no life in them. Now it was happening to him. A son was wanted as the heir to the throne, and this boy could have turned the road of history.

When Edward the Sixth died, all the world had known that he could not live very long for he was riddled with the disease which had killed his grandfather, his own father, and uncle, and when the clock struck, would kill him also.

Then, so Tom told himself, he could have pressed his heir forward, his *son*. But not a daughter. There were two other daughters standing first, Mary, with her evil eyes, her prim talk and her hardness, and Elizabeth, a wild girl, a girl with coarse red hair like her father had had. His blue eyes. His commanding presence also.

He did not trust Elizabeth.

'A daughter?' he asked desperately. For perchance he had dreamt it.

'A daughter, Sir.'

He turned away.

'Another girl? My God!' he thought, for there were far too many of them, Mary, Elizabeth, Mary of Scotland, and now *his* daughter, too.

His wife turned to look at him; it had been a difficult birth, and her face was white as a sheet. He thought that the stench of the sick chamber sickened him, for he detested charcoal, even if it eased his wife's pain. Now a cold sweat clung to her brow and she was pale as death. Even her mouth was the same colour as her cheeks, and he stood there looking down at her, not knowing what to say.

When at last he *did* speak, he said the wrong thing.

'A *daughter*,' he told her.

The poor lady made a courageous attempt to steady herself. 'The next time, your babe shall be the son you desire! I also,' she promised him.

'Of course, my dearest, yes, of course,' and he hardly knew how he came to say it.

Much later that evening, when poor Katherine had slept a little, and felt better for it, it was Jane who came down the stone stairs in a courageous attempt to soothe his grief. There were at the moment far too many girls coming close to the throne of England, with a claim to that throne, she realized. If Edward died unwed, then Mary would come after him, then to Elizabeth, and last of all possibly to herself.

She shuddered at the thought of being so near to it. A goose walked over my grave, she told herself sadly.

She was herself desperately fatigued with all that she had been through, and she had never thought that birth could be so agonizing or so cruel. Now she wished to assuage Seymour's grief, for he had so wanted a son. It was later than she had thought, but in the courtyard she could hear the watchman going the rounds, and calling out the time of night. Any signs of the dinner had gone, and the place was tidy.

She thought that all had gone to bed, for the place was so still, and now realized that she was not alone in the dining-hall. At first she thought that it must be one of the servants, sick with hunger, who had sneaked down here to filch food with which to silence the wicked qualms within them. She slipped behind a screen. It was then that she saw that a tall, well-dressed man was standing there, and it was Thomas Seymour himself. He looked changed. There was something different about him, something which gave her a sense of alarm, and of doubt. She did not run to him saying, 'It's me! It is Ja—nie, I came down here to see how you were!'

Some inner intuition took command of her and restraint, and held her back.

Now, keeping so still that she hardly recognized herself, she observed that in his hand he held a glass. There was a yellow fluid in it, the light from the tall sconces which held the tapers, showed it to her, like yellow topaz! He hesitated, glanced around him, almost as though he were half-afraid, then he brought out of his own velvet money bag (as did all gentlemen of the period), a small packet. He felt it with his fingers, to make sure of the contents she thought, and then paused again.

The girl could not imagine what he would be doing (and at this time of night, for she had anticipated that he would have gone to bed to recover from the anxiety through which he had passed). Now he opened the small packet. It was slender and flat; she had seen packages like them which one obtained from the chemistry men, who made up a potion for one.

None of this is true, she told herself. It is all something that I am dreaming, something that I do not understand.

She had never liked Thomas Seymour, which was strange, for most women adored him, and thought of him as being some handsome lover, a charmer, who could win their hearts. But he would never win *her* heart! From what she had seen of him here in the house, she knew that he could be a most dangerous flirt, had a savage temper when roused, and was too good looking to escape the vanity which good looks carry with them. She saw him push the last spot of powder out of the scrap of parchment which had held it, into the glass which had a golden fluid in it. He held the glass up to the light, and stared at it! She saw it too, brilliantly bright, and golden as are such fluids (some wine, perchance).

My God! But what is it that he does? she asked herself, and at that very moment became aware of the fact that she had lost control of her limbs. She was a spectator, a fly on the wall, little more. If she had wanted to call to him and stay him, she could not have done so. He poured water on the drink, shook it, and then it was that she heard him laugh. He laughed gaily, with some defiance in it, almost as though he could do whatever he wished with the world. Almost as if he were a king.

He turned.

Now was the moment that she should stay him, she knew, for he was moving away from her, towards the three stone steps which led out of this room into the hall, and on to the stairs which went to the floor above them. She should say that she had seen the mixture he was preparing; ask for whom it was intended, and what it was; yet she did nothing of the sort. She was sickly afraid!

He went up the three stone steps.

He went to them, lifting the heavy velvet

curtain, went beyond it, and she heard it fall again, swishing like a small wave breaking on the shore, and there arose a small cloud of dust.

Although the palace servants were clever, and worked hard, it was impossible to keep the houses spick and span. The straw on the floors picked up dirt, the heavy curtains were never shaken year in year out, dirt was not recognized as it is in the modern times. It was part of one's existence, and was for ever there.

Men and women slept in their day clothes, frequently in their shoes. Only the very aristocratic changed for the night. A mere swish of a brush was sufficient as a cleansing.

The cooking of meals had to be good, for they appreciated that cooking was urgent to the appetite. Nobody worried too much about dirt. It was ever here, one tolerated it.

She paused, and then she heard the sound of his footfalls on the stairs, going up them! He would be going to the Queen's room, for although Katherine was no longer a Queen, somehow they had all got into the habit, and alluded to her as being this. The girl had the feeling that there was a strange foreboding about this, something that she did not understand and that it was dangerous. As though death jogged at her side. *'Have a care I am here!'* Death warned her.

She did not know what to do.

She went out of the dining-hall and into the

hallway beyond it, which was ghostly in the purple splendour of the night. She could hear the sound of the tide coming in, for the river lay close to the house and the whispering of its tides was for ever with them, like some sort of lullaby. Suddenly the awful thought struck her that death would be here in this house before the hour of high tide! Was Seymour going to kill the babe, the unwanted girl, poor wee one?

He had gone ahead, two steps at the time, and she followed clumsily, for she was heavy for want of sleep; a growing girl who needed a full night of even sleep to help her grow into a woman.

She saw him go into the Queen's room, still carrying the container, which held some sort of potion which he had put together here for her.

Perhaps it was something to do the patient good, and make her better? Why had she ever allowed herself to imagine that it was poison; that fear was here, in the house with her, and death very close? Why had she thought such silly things? Yet the suspicion would not die for her. The man was very quiet, far quieter than he should be, she felt, and the Queen—poor lady!—was possibly asleep. A nurse had taken the little babe from the room, and was sleeping with her on the other side of the palace, where, if she woke and cried, she would not disturb her mother.

As she waited, Jane prayed.

Was she doing the right thing, in suspecting that this man, whom dear Katherine loved with such devotion, was behaving badly? If Katherine trusted him implicitly (and she did) then Jane *was* wrong. Yet she had seen him coquetting with the Princess Elizabeth; she had seen him go to her room at night, to kiss her good night, and his hand had slipped under the covering. She had seen Princess Elizabeth flush scarlet with rage, and had heard the resounding slap that she had given him. Once even she had turned, and had deliberately bitten his hand! Next day it was bound up, and Jane heard him tell the poor Queen that he had torn it on a rose branch which he had tried to tie up.

The rose branch had been the teeth of the Princess Elizabeth, and the girl knew it. There had been that last time when she herself had seen Tom Seymour lifting the Princess Elizabeth into the saddle and then his hand had gone too high. Instantly, the princess, furiously angry, had lifted her booted foot, and had kicked him full in the face with it. He had fallen down into the mud beside the horse! The men had come and had carried him away, and for a whole week he had not dared appear at meals saying that he had the toothache! But, when he did appear, there was still the light sign of the mark which was known in the household as being 'The Princess's footprint'.

Thomas Seymour loved women. That one

had to appreciate, and he had married poor Katherine because she was a queen, and not all men can wed a queen. Now he had gone into his wife's room, where he had the perfect right to be, without a doubt. *Every right!*

I have fear. I know something is wrong, and do not know what I should do, the girl told herself.

The moonlight drifted into the great hall, pale blue with here and there the reflection of a saffron tinged it with gold. She sat down on the lowest stair of them all. She did not know what happened, whether she fell asleep there, for it was a long time past her bedtime, or if she imagined things, but she woke suddenly, to find that her body had stiffened a little! This is madness, she thought. A man has the right to be in his wife's bedroom, for this is marriage, and why am I doubting him? She went to her own room.

I fell asleep on the stairs, and must to bed, she told herself.

She awakened with the dawn of a brilliant new day flooding the room with its brightness, and the scent of flowers. She lay there, not quite sure of herself, with that strangely remote sensation which comes with waking, and then dimly, and far away, she heard the sound of a bell tolling. A bell? she asked herself. A bell for someone dead, but who can it be? and she sprang up.

She got to the door just as the little maid entered and came in.

'That bell?' Jane gasped, and knew that she had gone white as death.

The girl told her. 'It is the Dowager Queen,' she said, and her face was swollen with weeping. 'She fell asleep, and died *in* her sleep.'

'But why should she die? She was recovering last night? The birth was over and she was well.'

'She died! The babe also,' said the girl.

'The babe also? But the babe was not ill,' and Jane knew that her voice had changed. 'Something ... someone ...' then remembering Seymour only last night, she fainted.

She woke in her room lying on the bed.

She knew of course, the truth. Seymour had killed his wife. He had seen perchance a bigger prize ahead of him, and had had no mercy. She learnt that the Queen had suffered what appeared to be a small convulsion, and never regained consciousness. Nobody had wakened Jane, for Seymour had told them not to do so! She knew when the maid told her this that it had been intentional. My God! she told herself.

He came to sympathize with her.

'Do not fret too deeply, my sweet Jane,' he said, 'for Katherine was old to have her first child, we ought to have foreseen the danger,' and then half-teasingly, 'weep not, for you will lose your pretty colour if you do, and you are to be a bridesmaid at your cousin Anne Seymour's marriage.'

'I cannot do that,' she said. 'I cannot possibly attend a marriage so quickly after a funeral.'

He pressed her hand. 'Time is the great healer,' was what he said, and she noted the roguishness in his eyes as he touched her.

'But, one *remembers*,' she told him.

He looked at her with doubt in his eyes. Perhaps he guessed the truth!

SEVEN

The jewel that we find, we stop and take it,
Because we see it, but what we do not see
We tread upon, and never think of it.
                                    William Shakespeare

THE day of Anne Seymour's marriage was a brilliant one. It was at Isleworth, and a fair spot for any marriage to be. Here the gentle river curved graciously, coming to the shore, and chuckling at low tide as it whispered against the stones, and the wreckage which high tide had left behind it there.

Jane was staying at Syon House, with her uncle, the demanding Lord Northumberland, and he had curious plans for the future.

During this summer the health of the young King had deteriorated badly. Edward had been a weak babe, but devotedly nursed by old Nurse Penn. By seven years of age he was quite a sturdy little boy, and extremely clever at book learning. Now he had some strange malady, a fever of sorts which did not respond to the doctors' treatment. He had been a stout child, and he began losing weight. His colour which had been high, changed to a yellowness which was like wild groundsel in a cabbage patch, some said.

Looking at the boy now, he had changed so much that one hardly believed that he would ever reign when he reached eighteen years of age. Could it be that the dread malady which had mown down the Tudors one after the other, had come to him, and the scythe of Death the Reaper, now moved in his direction?

He had lost his vivid likeness to his father, and had become more as his gentle mother had been, who died giving him birth. He was in fact, a Seymour.

Northumberland played his cards well, determined to win in this game of life. Maybe it was the period when strategy was the secret of success. Men fought to maintain their position and he fought for the crown.

The shattering of the Catholic church had falsified many of the most absolute beliefs, and whereas at one period, all men had believed that in earth one laid up storage for the reward in Heaven (or naturally, his curse in Hell), this had gone! The Church had weakened, and avarice was stronger than ever before.

Poor little Jane had been shattered when kind Katherine Parr had died and so mysteriously, she felt that she had lost her best friend, and now she returned to her own people, for she had lost touch with them, and found them unscrupulous, plotting, and strangely alien to her.

The young King, although a minor, was very prompt with opinions, and showed signs of having his late father's command when older. *If* he grew older! All manner of strange rumours were going around the country as to his death before he came of age.

'But if I die, I will first produce the new prayer book,' he told his cousin, and he meant this. He felt that this mission had been entrusted to him by his dead father, and—if he should die, as he felt he easily might do—then his sister, Elizabeth, must carry one. He cut out his elder sister, violently Catholic in her principles, and against the new Church, on which his dead father had been so intent. The Princess Mary had the good sense never to shun the young King, to be well behaved and prudent in her behaviour to him if they met, for ever curtseying and being loyal outwardly, but he had the feeling that she was the girl who would bide her time. Then ... what. . . . ?

'If Mary comes to the throne,' he told Jane,

'the fires at Tyburn will burn again, and the block at The Tower be eternally scarlet with the blood of good men and true.'

Perhaps the whole of England had never been in such a quandary as it was now, the young King sick (even more so than his doctors believed) and standing behind this poor young King four women who were his heirs. Mary and Elizabeth, Jane and the Queen of Scotland.

'But, have courage, Jane,' he told the girl, 'God helps us. I shall endow the throne of England to neither of my sisters, since each in her turn has been condemned as being a bastard. I shall leave it to you, and pray you to guard it and to treat the people kindly.'

'But you must *not* die.'

He had laughed at that. 'No man asks to die, but in the end, this unwelcome visitor comes to each of us,' he said.

'But not to you, Edward! Your life is so badly needed—not to you.'

He kissed her. 'Death comes to all men and is the uninvited guest,' was what he said. 'Go as bridesmaid to Anne, and be happy at the marriage feast.

★   ★   ★

Jane went to the wedding. She was now thirteen years of age, a woman or almost so the world thought. It was a glorious day and she looked at the crooked houses of Isleworth, the inn at the water's edge, and the old church. A pleasant green garden lay round it, where men and women slept their last sleep, and late buttercups still showered abundance, bluebells with them, stonecrop and late cowslips.

She was excited as she waited.

May Day had come and had gone again, and what a day it had been! It was the green festival of noble spring, a May Queen and love. Across the ripple of the Thames lay the fields of Surrey, also in pale gold, and near them the gardens of Syon House, with lilacs scenting the air, and the laburnums shaking golden tassels.

Jane had changed.

At this time she had lost her dearest friend in the late Queen, and when she had seen her friend die she felt that her childhood had ended. Still a child in years, grief had laid a hand on her, and she knew that this death had been devised by the man, whom poor Katherine had married. Poor, poor Katherine! She had been wife to four separate men and not one of them had been good husbands. She had seldom known joy. I grieve for her, was the kindly girl's constant thought.

Now she was growing up quickly.

She had a Tudor rose embroidered on her girdle, and some of them in little bunches in her hair. She was a pretty girl, not beautiful, but she had sad eyes. she wished that 'Uncle Harry' had never died. Strangely enough she had perhaps cared for him more than others had done.

Waiting at the waterside, she thought what a great age thirteen years was to be, for many of her little friends had married when they were but eleven years old, and most of them plighted. Privately she was a little afraid lest Uncle Northumberland had made any secret plans for her, for this was usually his method. And those plans usually helped him himself far more than the niece or nephew in question. She wished Queen Katherine had lived. She wished that she were not so alone.

She thought of cousin Edward, and how happy the hours which she had been allowed to spend with him, had always been. She thought of Cousin Bess, Anne Boleyn's daughter, and a friend. But Edward was the one she loved.

The barge came up beside the shallow water, and opposite was the pretty spot with the cluster of silvery willow trees on it, and the brackish scent of the water itself. It was the strong smell of the river. Now she saw the royal barge coming up stream from Hampton Court Palace with the King's pennant flying from it, a flash of vivid colour, and she knew that she would travel with him to the marriage of their cousins at Richmond.

He came nearer and she saw he wore cream velvet. Hot, for such a day, for now the sun was powerful, lacing the world with gold and with crystal. The barge drew level, and the girl approaching the King, curtseyed to the ground.

'Good day, my coz.' Edward had a gay boyish voice, and he laughed. He was young enough, and—for the moment—well enough to enjoy a day which he could spend away from his tutors and such, who, at times, he believed had the capacity to drive him mad.

'God be with you, sweet, my coz!' she said.

'Bless you, Jane,' and the boat came nearer.

'You also, my lord, my kinsman, and my King.'

One of the sailors gave her a hand, a strong man's hand, severely roughened by hard work, and brine, as are the hands of all men of the sea. He helped the girl into the boat, and, for a single moment, just as she strode across the narrow inlet of water, a mere ditch between herself and the shore, she wobbled badly, then scrambled into the barge and took her place beside His Grace. He greeted her gladly.

'And how is my fair Jane, this day?' he asked her smiling.

'I am right well, Sire, and glad of a holiday with no lessons to do, lines to remember, and work set aside to do tonight, because this morn it was not satisfactory.'

'For me, the same. No lessons today,' and they laughed together. He said, 'They teach me the most boring lessons, and although I tell them that they wear me out and fatigue me, they do not listen.'

'You are the King.' She laughed as she said it. 'Tell them that you will not have it!'

He shook his head.

'But Kings are boys as well as others, and when we are young we learn how to live life. I work hard now. The new prayer book is almost ready, and is the joy of my life, for this would have made my respected father so very glad.'

'It would indeed, Sire,' she agreed, 'but you need rest, amusement, dancing, parties! All of us need happiness.'

He shook his head. 'Jane, Kings have to work harder than any other men! Learn more than they do, and I believe that every good King knows this.'

'You will kill yourself with overwork, Sire.'

He laughed, almost as though such a thing were impossible. 'If I indeed do that, my coz, then I have anyway done my duty! We have today, and today is sweet. It is summer weather, and we are here to enjoy it together.' He put out a pitifully thin hand, and touched her own.

Arriving at Richmond, they were met by the town, an enormous crowd of people, the bells of the churches ringing gladly; everywhere flags flew, and the Tudor Rose blossomed in abundance. They went on to the church and there the young girl joined the others of the bride's retinue, whilst the boy was escorted to the improvised throne which had been set to one side for him. It was a tedious service, with too much singing; later they adjourned to the great house for celebrations.

What a brilliant day it was, but the heat tired the young King so that for a while he had to adjourn to a bedroom, already prepared lest this happened, for he suffered from bad faints. He lay down for a time, with only the sound of distant music, *Greensleeves*, his favourite tune, and he recovered so that later he felt better and came down to supper. And what a supper it was, with a royal swan taking the centre place at the table, with chickens and capons, with ducklings and such!

The meal would last for three to four hours, and if longer that was not exceptional. Wine was poured down the guests, there were dancers giving exhibitions, and soothsayers to predict the happy future, and many children for the young couple.

Then, as the evening progressed, and midnight struck, there came the strict formula of seeing the young couple to bed. How amusing a marriage could be! How entertaining for the guests; if some felt their modesty to be estranged, then that was because they were over-sensitive, for all the world knew that the ordination of marriage was to produce children to follow in the parental footsteps.

The bridesmaids and the bride's old nurse, helped undress the girl herself, already exhausted by the ceremony and the rites, the food and wine, the fortune-telling and the eternal music. Then, when ready, they escorted the bride in procession, now wearing the exquisitely embroidered chemise, specially made for her wedding night, and at the door of the prepared bridal chamber, she met the bridegroom with his retinue of young gentlemen friends awaiting her.

The priests blessed the bed, and they were escorted to it. One by one the guests departed, some giggling, some slightly shocked, others dismayed, but all of them heady with the rich wine which had been running ever since the marriage feast began, and which now had dulled some, but had made others more lively.

Jane returned in the barge for Syon, leaving at midnight, and she had fallen asleep before the great house came into sight, standing back from the water, and shimmering in the blue light of the moon. Another little bridesmaid curled, half-asleep, beside her, said, 'I would not wed for all the world! What happens now?'

'They are happy.' Jane said.

'But are they happy? Who would dare say they were unhappy, when they were not? Who? Who?'

'They *are* happy!' Jane repeated.

She knew that the thought of marriage was in the air, for marriage bells beget other peals of marriage bells, and somehow today she had realized that already her parents and guardians must have discussed her own marriage.

Guildford Dudley had watched her closely. It had been suggested to him by his own family that at this particular time, the throne and the crown, which went with it, were veering in Jane's direction. Those in power looked on such an alliance with approval

The Princess Mary might be counted out of the ruling, for somehow now, with the new Church taking definite shape and place, the Roman Catholicism of previous days was losing power. People were more lax. The Princess was harsh; she had had a terrible life, wronged by her father, and destined to see the mother (to whom she was devoted), die wretchedly, and it had possibly warped the girl herself. One could exclude her. The Princess Elizabeth had been reckoned as a bastard, and all her life had had this curse hanging over her. She was learned, well educated, and had spirit, but few forgave her mother for the wretchedness she had given to the Aragon Princess, who had died so wretchedly. Since Catholicism had faded a little, people had become less autocratic and more lazy. Elizabeth was too virulent to catch the imagination, and there was a rumour going the rounds of London, through the alleyways and little lanes, that the young King had left his throne and his crown to the third woman on the list of those entitled, and the third one was his cousin, the little Lady Jane Grey. Until now there had never been a woman reign, but now suddenly if this young king died, there would be four standing waiting for the crown. No son. Would it be the good girl, the scholar Jane?

Men discussed it in the brothels, and the inns. Jane might easily be the Queen if the King died before he could marry, and have sons of his own, and this *was* dubious! He was weak and frail, and growing frailer every day. Jane would be a good queen, and a righteous one. She was not flirtatious, perhaps too studious, but she had beauty, she had charm, and she would never have done man nor beast a bad turn. Undoubtedly, Northumberland had not overlooked this.

Young Guildford had inherited the family longing which had already made others lose their heads (the desire to do well for himself), and undoubtedly he would stop at very little to achieve this end. The throne had quavered. Henry the Seventh had been a bad king, and a mean one. Henry the Eighth had been a spendthrift, and a bad king. His son was too young and too ill to be anything, and this day, at the wedding, there had been moments when he had looked as if he were dying here and now.

'He is his father's own son,' some whispered, 'the same complaint.'

'Yes, indeed, the same, and he will never see manhood as all the world can see.'

How right they were and now the boy's hopes of life could be reckoned only in weeks, not days. It was the same thing which had happened to his Uncle Arthur, who had got as far as espousing the Princess of Aragon and then had died within a few weeks.

Guildford Dudley had to admit that he admired the girl, Jane, who was very pretty, though not actually beautiful. She was proficiently taught, was undoubtedly a scholar, which he was not, but he had to remember that it would be a royal marriage which had other joys to give to him (maybe the crown of England) and palaces to live in. But it would have dangers too, and this night he thought sadly of it. One could not dismiss those dangers too easily.

At Syon House the festivities and the entertainments were continued for a week, which gave the young man the chance to visit and meet Jane yet again. He found that her tutors had done their work well, but the seeds of learning which they had sown within her, had taken deep root! He talked with her. Together they watched the Morris men dancing on the green grass of the parkland, the knee bells making a merry music of their own and everyone clapped and applauded them.

He walked one afternoon, with the child, into the garden bright with flowers and the great park spreading belonging to it, where the deer grazed. In October, when the rutting season came, this park would be highly dangerous, he knew, but for now it was peaceful and fair.

'In autumn the deer are savage,' he told her.

'Why should they be?' she asked gently.

'That is the month when love moves them. Love makes demands of a man, and animals also. One day you yourself will be in love, and discover this.' He smiled at her.

She said timidly, 'I would be afraid to wed.'

'But why? Why? You could give a man great joy, a happiness which few other maids could offer. One day you yourself will be in love, and find how true this is.'

'I shall not wed,' she said, thoughtfully, 'unless it is ... unless,' and she coloured.

'Unless it is ... whom?'

She said quietly, 'I do love the King, my cousin.'

'He is charming, and clever too, but he has not long to live so they say; some reckon his future is the matter of weeks only, if not days.

She said, 'But why should he not live?'

'There is a secret malady which strikes the kings so they say. You must have heard of it? Henry the Seventh died of it, and his son Prince Arthur, died actually on his honeymoon of it. It is this same malady which laid the late King low, and now has touched his son. His *only* son.'

'Poor Uncle Henry! He was good to me and kind. He loved all children, as well I know.'

He spoke in a low voice. 'It is said that a curse has been laid upon the royal family, and they will never go from father to son for three full generations. Always this curse will stay them.'

'I have never heard of that before,' and she coloured nervously.

'They do say (but then the city always talks wildly) that the Tudor line is breaking now, and will end. That in the end we shall turn to Scotland for a king.'

'You mean Mary, the princess who is in France? The princess whom some say could, one day, be our Queen.'

He looked at her. He was good-looking, and she liked his fresh colouring, and bright eyes. 'We live in curious times, my sweet, and much must happen before we can put these matters right.'

She was thinking of what he had said, the four heirs waiting to come to this throne when the poor young King died! Mary, Elizabeth, herself, and the young girl who had married the Dauphin of France. It alarmed her unduly and she felt the sweat pearl her brow and hands, and wiped it away nervously.

'I do not wish to look ahead,' she said. 'I do not seek to be a queen myself, I would never want that, but I do seek that my cousin lives, and grows strong again. Then the throne is Mary's, and she . . . she can be hard.'

'The seers say that she will not live to see

forty.'

To the girl in the teens, forty was senility! 'That is old age,' she said and laughed.

'When you are thirty-nine, you will not think quite the same thing,' he told her, and he laughed. 'Maybe the hour will come when you go to the Stone of Scone. It could be.'

'I have no wish to be a queen.'

He kissed her then, very gently and she had to admit that the kiss did not displease her. He was a good-looking young man with a clear bright skin, amused eyes and crimson mouth which reminded her of poppies. His arms were warm, and strong about her.

'I love my cousin, the young King,' she whispered.

'The King will not live, and I shall! Already the poor lad is looking death in the eyes, whilst I am not. I have life before me, the chance to travel, to live well, to fight, and to *win*.' He laughed as he said it. She admired the vigorous youth which endowed him. He took her hand, and opening it laid it palm uppermost on his own. 'I see a crown in your hand, sweet Jane! It is the crown of England, and one day you will be the Queen of England. But now, I kiss your lips because you are queen of my own heart, and I love you.' He kissed her fondly, and she was surprised by the warmth of his lips, and the power he had to arouse in her such strong emotions. Maybe she was growing up, for other girls had told her that as one grew older, this happened, and one turned to love, reaching out one's hands to it.

She whispered, 'This is wrong.'

'No, it is right; it is right for us, and what we should do. I love you, Janie. I knew that I loved your gentleness, when your father first whispered of his plans for us.'

'His plans for *me*?' and she stared, dismayed.

He had, he knew then, spoken too quickly. Women were not the same as men, who approached a destination which they had had in sight and long before they reached it. Had others talked of her future, making plans for it which as yet had not materialized? It horrified her, for sooner or later, whatsoever she did, these plans would materialize.

'I have no desire to wed,' she whispered, her voice tremulous, 'I am afraid....'

He kissed her then and found her responsive. When she could not extricate herself from his arms, she brushed away the grass seed, and jerked her body away. Primly, she said that it was time they returned to the house, else they would be missed.

'Of course,' he said, and they went together. He had, he felt, made proud progress towards the fulfilment of his father's desires for him. His father saw the crown ahead of them, and wished above all else to retain it in his family. Love did not excite him, but riches and such *did*! He hoped to make his own son the consort to the Queen at the Abbey church one day and promised himself that he would achieve this end.

During the week suddenly the poor young King who had seemed to be better, had what his doctors called 'an acute attack' and gave few details. It was attributed to the fact that he had been overworking on the new prayer book, determined to get it accepted.

In those days the young studied, in a manner which would kill the modern child! All the young people were expected to dedicate themselves to learning from early dawn, until the last star faded at night. None were allowed to be lazy, and no apprehensions were suffered for them. Nobody ever concerned themselves that a child might overdo it, or that he or she needed time to play, time to enjoy themselves, for learning was essential to the early years, and all children studied hard.

In spite of his illness, the young King had suffered with this. Only old Nurse Penn maintained that hot rooms, and the airless conditions of learning his lessons, were bad for him and should not be! Now, during this 'attack' she was called back to the palace to be with him. She kept his tutors and masters out of his room, and nursed him day and night. She was now a very old woman, and people said that when she died, the King of England would die with her, which was probably true!

But as ever, she was prepared to fight death for him.

She had gathered him into her arms the moment that he was born, how well she remembered that! 'A boy, Your Grace, a king for England, and as pretty a Prince of Wales as ever any of us did see!' she had averred.

Now she knew that he had never been so seriously ill before. Day and night she stayed with him, and gradually brought him round, for the doctors admitted that she could do this which none of the others could achieve. She asked that Jane should visit him, but it so happened that she was unwell herself, and could not come.

She heard that there was better news, that the King was rounding the corner, coming through, and was better again. She could rely on Nurse Penn, she knew. What she did not know was that her own marriage was now being discussed closely. Guildford Dudley was not averse to espousing her. Like all his family he had burning pride born in him, and the desire to improve his position and go on ahead to greater gains. He liked the girl, their meeting had been a happy one. His family were anxious too. It was to them obvious that, when the King died, and he was now close to death itself, one could put on one side the two bastard daughters of the late King Henry the Eighth. Next on the list, and rightful heir after him, was Lady Jane Grey, and after her the Scottish Princess. If one wished to claim the crown the thing to do was for Guildford to wed Jane, who was next on the list, and the time was now.

Jane wondered why the hours she spent on study were being so relaxed. Always before she had been hard driven, never excused, but now she had time to walk in the park, and to gather flowers and the man who came with her was ever Guildford.

In these weeks the plans were laid, and the dice thrown by the men in power. None thought twice of what could happen to the little girl, whose fate was in the balance, and she, for her part, trusted them. Yet again, the King rallied.

He had inherited that extraordinary power to rally when almost at the gate of death itself. The summer died calmly; autumn was mild, and then there came a January which was cold as steel. Seymour was working hard to get his foot set inside the door, and his son wed to the heir to the throne. The Protector took action. He knew that he faced a man determined to get his own way, and one who would fight for the throne to the bitter end. A hard frost had set in, coming with the biting wind when the Protector took action, and Seymour went to The Tower on January the 16th.

As his barge approached Traitor's Gate, and he saw that fatal dark arch above the water, icicles hanging from the arch, he knew all hope had gone. The Tower never returned guests who entered by this route.

He hàd behaved vilely of course, eternally harbouring plans against his brother, and now this was the man who actually signed the warrant for his execution. The young King rallied, and had had a better bout than he had had in the summer; then he had come closer to his death than ever before.

This is not my good new year Seymour had thought. He little knew how accurate was his conjecture.

★   ★   ★

Whilst this tumult continued, this horror of family raging against family, half England aching to replace a Catholic on the throne, the other half longing for the Protestant girl, whom they felt should succeed her brother, when he died, the little Lady Jane Grey was returned to the custody of her parents, and she went back to Leicestershire. Once more she was with pastors and masters, working hard, and saying that she got more enjoyment from reading Plato than she could ever get from playing with other maidens in the fields.

In the May of 1551, there is a letter written by her tutor, after she had spent a time with him at Bradgate. He admired her deeply.

For my own part I do not think that there ever lived anyone more deserving of respect, than this young lady, if you regard her family; more learned, if you consider her age, or more happy if you consider so. A report has prevailed that this most noble citizen is to be betrothed, and to be given in marriage to the King's Majesty. Oh, if that event should take place, how happy would be the union, and how beneficial to the Church.

What he said was probably quite true.

In Leicestershire, Jane was now fifteen years of age, and she had begun to see a little beyond her daily lessons. Life was intriguing her. She had always known that she was in sequence to the throne, but never for a moment would she have suggested that she should take precedence before her Uncle Henry's two daughters. Now, this was explained to her.

One April night, when she was going to her room to prepare for the night, a message came to her from her mother, telling her that her father must see her immediately. She had actually begun to undo her gown, when she got the message, hooked it together again and then went downstairs to the door of her father's library. A page waited for her, he had been lounging on the form which was sat outside the door for him, and, seeing her, he sprang up, colouring violently.

He opened the door for her, and she entered, paused to drop the submissive curtsey which was her duty, and typical of the good manners of her time. Her father was sitting there looking very worn and tired, she thought, and she wondered if he had received bad news from the palace which he was now about to tell her.

He spoke calmly.

'My daughter, you will be wondering why it is that I have sent for you, but as you must have realized for some time now, I have been contemplating your marriage.'

She looked at him, dismayed that he should send for her at this time of night to tell her this. Surely the news could have waited till the morning? She paused, curtseyed again, and then informed him that indeed she *had* been aware of it. He spoke very calmly to her. In complete control of his emotions as she saw, she said that he had conversed with the Duke of Northumberland who was the power behind the throne, and to whose integrity the family owed much. Then he paused, obviously nervous, and not quite sure of the ground on which he trod. In a weaker voice he spoke again.

'Jane, dear child, you do understand, I hope, that one day the throne, and the crown could come to you?'

Until this moment the young girl had not appreciated how dismayed she was by the thought of all it would mean to her. Possibly, for some months now, she had realized that poor Edward could never hope to reach his majority. He had taken serious turns for the worse, and did not recover as completely as before. Now there was a distracting period when he could not rise from his bed, because of the feverish tremor which possessed him. The boy was fighting the enemy which had destroyed others of his family, and it was a losing fight. She knew the family were distracted as to what would happen when he died, for there might be civil risings.

'It could be very difficult,' her father said.

'I see that, Sire.'

'But you are the rightful one. Both the other girls have been announced as being bastards.'

Mary *was* heir to the throne without a doubt, but, if she came to that throne, she would reinstate Catholicism as everyone knew. There would be an age of constant burnings and beheadings, something too horrible even to contemplate. The new faith was a kinder, more placid one, than the old faith had been, and did not bow to interference from Rome which the old one had done. The Catholics were still forceful, and the princess would be forceful.

Time and distress had changed Mary considerably. There had been a time when poor Jane Seymour had died in her arms, and she had been goodness itself to her. When she had carried the four-day-old prince to his baptism in Hampton Court Palace chapel, and had rejoiced in the fact that, at last the country had a prince who would succeed his father. She had been good to her father in his last illness, and had helped his sixth queen, but after that, she had changed bitterly.

She had opposed the Protestant Church violently, and nothing would stem that shocking tidal wave of cruelty which it had roused within her. Possibly, and the young Lady Jane knew it, Mary Tudor was one of the most difficult women in history to understand, that is if anyone ever *did* understand her.

It was understandable that none wished to see her on the throne, knowing full well what it could mean to others. But the King was nearing death. Her father faced Jane.

She said, 'I always pray Sir, that the King whom we all love, will throw aside this dreadful malady and recover.'

'It is alas, a malady men do *not* fling aside! He is worse, I have the gravest news of his condition now, and undoubtedly it is only a matter of months, perhaps weeks, before it kills him.'

She went very white, and felt the tears burning behind her eyes. 'I shall still pray for him, Sir, and hope.'

He paused, giving her the chance to recover and then he said. 'When Edward dies, what do you suppose will happen?'

'I ... I expect that the Princess Mary has made arrangements, and that she will come to the throne.'

He spoke sternly then. It was against the wishes of the whole world that this should happen, for nobody wanted her on the throne, seeing the vengeance and the period of terror she would bring with her. She would bring back the old faith, and for this, many more would die. It was true that there was another candidate, the Princess Elizabeth at the moment at Hatfield House, but on the whole, it would probably be better for the country in the long run to turn away from these two daughters, and look to the third girl standing in the line for the throne.

Jane was that third.

'I—I have no wish to be the Queen of England, Sir,' she said quietly.

'But you must desire to save your country from Papist rule, and the horror which it could bring.'

'I wish to help my country sir, and do all in my power for the people here, but I have no right to step on to the throne to which Mary is the true heiress, and comes first.'

'You realize that Henry the Eighth himself declared that both of his daughters were bastards?'

She said, 'I know there ... there was something of that kind, but it was not true! Mary was his daughter, without a doubt, and stands next for the throne.'

Her father was furiously angry with her then, and raged against her. She stood there trembling a little, but quite calm in the face of his most passionate resentment; when he had finished what he had to say, and realized that it had not done what he had expected of it, he paused again. He began on another subject.

'It is essential that you should wed, Jane.'

She had never thought that her own marriage could, in any way, help the young King who was dying, and she said so timidly.

He told her, 'I have spoke of this to the Duke of Northumberland.'

'Yes, sir.'

'He is a great power and a wise man, and this very day he has asked for your hand in marriage with his son, Guildford Dudley.'

Somehow it did not surprise her, for she had wondered several times if this idea might not lurk behind the secrets of this court. She paled; then she faltered that she hardly knew the young man.

'I hardly knew your mother,' her father told her, 'when our marriage was arranged for us, and we have been very happy.'

'I know that you have,' she said.

'We all know the young man, and I do not think that you could expect to get a better husband. I wish you to understand that I and your mother want this.' He paused, then he said, 'The marriage will take place in May.'

The girl stared at him, the world spinning round her, and she herself, a little dizzily, struggling to keep her balance in it. She said, 'Yes sir,' and was ashamed when she realized how cold was the tone of her voice, and the dread which raised a spike-like growing desire within her. She felt herself distrusted.

She faltered for a moment, not daring to look her father in the face, and when she could speak, she said humbly, 'I hardly know the gentleman. We have met once or twice, no more. I would not say that I knew him.'

For a moment her father did not speak, having expected her to be enchanted by the suggestion, and thought that her mother had prepared her for this big step into the future, and on eventually to the throne itself, the prize, on which he had had his eye, for some long time.

He looked at her. Then he spoke again. 'Love is not the main urgency in marriage. Often the quiet alliance, which starts with the two people hardly knowing one another, matures into the most beautiful alliance of true happiness. A pair gets to know one another in the everyday living of life! You must not expect much at first, when both of you are almost strangers.'

'But sir,' and her face showed how troubled the poor child was. She had always idealized the Sacrament of marriage, believing it to be beyond this world, a position in which two people were eternally happy together, and when joy came so great!

Her father was losing his temper (he had always been quick-tempered) and now he was feeling an inner fury squirming with him, anger that this girl had the ignorance of the future, and the disobedience to question his right to dictate to her. He had ordained for her a really wonderful marriage, with the crown round the next corner, and he visualized himself as the father of the Queen, given all those extra liberties, and favours, to which only the father of the Queen was permitted. He spoke sharply!

'This is a very promising young man, and the eyes of the world are on his future. He is good-looking, many girls would be grateful for a glance from that handsome face of his. He is nineteen years of age when you are just fifteen, which is the right age for both of you. You do not realize to what work your people have been put on your behalf nor the great prize which lies ahead for you.'

'I do not seek great prizes,' she said simply.

He was growing madly impatient with her, and could not bear any more of it. He had never thought for a single moment of the maid being disobedient, a bad quality in any maid, and it shocked him. More that it was so unexpected; most girls, if you had told them you had plans ahead when one of the most handsome young men at court, was prepared to wed them, and the throne of the country come to them with all its blessings, and all his power, would have screamed for sheer joy. He had half anticipated hysterics of happiness, but not this. He looked at her, saw that her eyes were brimming with tears, and then very nervously, she confessed her anxiety.

'I am afraid...' she said.

'There is no need to be. None at all. I promise you that this will be a good marriage which the world will envy, and you will hold a position of power which will make you the star of Europe.'

Hardly understanding what he said, she answered again, 'I am afraid, still very much afraid.....!'

'It will be a good marriage, and even if you are slightly young, at fifteen all girls are fit to be wives if they so wish. All the three brides who will wed on the same day (for I have already made my plans) will be young. Your sister, Katherine, will be with you marrying Lord Herbert.'

Aghast with surprise, she said, 'I ... I did not know ... I thought that it was not to be.'

'You thought wrongly. Parents make marriages for the families and at the same ceremony, Lady Katherine Dudley will marry Lord Hastings as is arranged.'

She knew of course that a long time before the plans had been made for her. This had been the secret which her parents were keeping ever since her cradle. First it was to be the King himself, and she had been enchanted by the thought. Poor Edward needed someone to support him, help him, and comfort him, and she would be enchanted to do this. But recently his health had deteriorated so dreadfully, that they saw, and surely all the world would see that this was a marriage which would never be, for the young bridegroom would be in Heaven when the hour came.

She knew instinctively that by now her father would have found another bridgegroom, and Dudley was the man whom he had chosen for her. There could be no escape. The father of a family was the master and could rule if he so wished. Her own marriage lay in his hands; he chose the groom for her, and it was her duty to obey him. The condition of the poor young King was worsening and swiftly. His life was coming to its end. The moment her parents discovered this, they changed their tactics. When the hour came, who would follow this king to the Stone of Scone, and to his crowning? Not Mary, for her Catholicism would stay this. Not Elizabeth, for she had been declared illegitimate.

She said, 'Forgive me, Father, and be patient with me, for I have no wish to displease you, and would serve you. I have a little time in which I can recover, then I shall be ready and willing to pursue whatever rules you have set out for me, and will do as you desire.'

He said blankly, and with the brutal truth which had actually forced his hand at this moment, and against which his wife had already warned him. 'My hand is being forced. I cannot choose the moment, nor the hour,' and his voice jerked slightly, 'I only know that life gives us chances, great, rich opportunities which none but a fool would dismiss.'

'I know, sir. I know.'

'We have got to lay hold of life, whilst the world is ours. Look ahead, Jane, not now! Look ahead, and take your courage in your hands.'

Somehow she guessed that everything had been prepared for her, and there was no possibility of escape. If the condition of the poor King worsened, and the doctors had taken it upon themselves to warn those most concerned, then death lay round the next corner, the boy could not last, then everything would change and she would have to agree to do what he said.

'There will be a triple marriage,' he told her, 'and this is too late in the day to recede from it. And you will wed Dudley.'

'I . . . I hardly know him, my father. . . .'

'You will get to know him, that should be easy,' and he laughed. 'It is not the first time that a girl has made a most brilliantly happy marriage, and to her amazement, does it, believing it would never be happy, to find how wrong she was!'

'I could be wrong, Father,' and now the tears came. 'I am very much afraid.'

'No need at all. No need,' and he rose. There was no escape for her, for the whole thing had been arranged and settled within these very walls, and such a successful marriage, when the girl came to the throne, would mean that success would come to her father! Jane must wed before her cousin, the young King, died, for this would give her a tremendous advantage over the other two candidates for the throne, the Princesses Mary, and Elizabeth. He had too quick an eye for points of any gain to himself, to miss details.

'You shall be happy,' he said.

'Yes, sir.' She spoke coldly, her voice quivering a little, for she felt as one who is numbed by the icy blast of some hopeless hurricane which rising from nothing, ruins a hundred lives, and then goes back to peace again! She made a last effort.

'I hardly know anything of him, Father, because there has been no time. Neither of us has been alone together to talk for more than half a dozen times, if that, nor have we had any opportunity to discover if, by chance, we loved one another, or not.'

'Love is no recipe for happy marriage.' The man's voice was getting sharp; it had a cutting power in it, which she knew well, and dreaded most dismally. He was getting sick of this stupid girl and her stubbornness, sick of the fact that she dare say the idea was not good, when it was quite the best idea in England for the actual moment! The man was nineteen, the right age for a girl of fifteen, of course, and he was good-looking. He could argue no further for this ended it.

He rose angrily, a man standing there in a silver embossed gown, made of purple velvet, and soft to the touch. A jewelled necklace of square cut amethysts, hung round his throat, and low.

'You will marry the young man,' he said. 'You must do what your father dictates,' and his voice was harsh.

She curtseyed beautifully and low to him. 'Yes, sir.'

There was nothing else that she could say, and she knew it. She admitted that she had liked the gay young man when they had met, admiring his good looks, his beautiful figure, and his complete understanding of what to do and how to do it. He was a genius at court etiquette.

'What does the King say, my lord?' she asked her father.

'The King is too ill to be troubled with things of this kind, but he would give his blessing.'

'You are sure, sir?'

'Of course I am sure,' but somehow she knew that he had lied to her.

At the very thought of the King her eyes

brimmed over. He was so near to death, that none should bother him about herself, he had other and far greater things to think of. Without a doubt she would go to that wedding, the eldest of the three brides, and she, but fifteen years of age. If she appealed to her mother, she would be treated sharply, she realized, for all women were under their husbands' thumbs, and must try to do as they were told.

Then hope, the guardian angel of all young people quivered into her life. Supposing that a miracle happened and the beloved young King recovered again, what then? The last time that she had seen him he appeared to have shrunk almost to skin and bones, shocking her with his skeleton thinness. But miracles did exist.

She curtseyed, and left her father.

He had dismissed her proudly believing that he had done his duty and with wisdom, and his daughter was the luckiest lady in all England. She went to her own room, knowing that she would marry Dudley, and she felt as though she walked through a dream, a mystifying one.

What lies ahead? she asked herself.

PART TWO

What is a king? A man condemned to bear
The public burden of the nation's care.
Matthew Prior

EIGHT

> And ever since historian writ
> And ever since a bird could sing,
> Doth man exalt with all his wit
> The noble art of murdering.
>
> *Thackeray*

THE triple marriages took place at Durham House, and the day was warmly radiant; none could have wished for better or a fairer omen for the future. There was much public interest in the dress and the festivities; the giving away of cake and wine to the poor, and the generous abundance with which guests were entertained and fêted.

It had, of course, been necessary that there should be nothing of the hole-in-the-corner treatment of this marriage, for they desired that everyone should know about it.

Guildford Dudley was a good-looking young man, something of a fop, and suffering perchance from too much flattery by nurses, and his mother. He was ambitious, eloquent, and amusing. He could make love with the true gallantry of the period, for men boasted of the way they filched a maiden's virtue, laughed, and then ran away. The love of the day was free and easy. Henry the Eighth had brought this code into fashion and because to many it was an agreeable code, they adhered to it amiably.

The bride was good, quiet, and a virgin. She was obedient to her parents, believing that she had no right to assert herself, not that she would have done had she had the right. Her whole life had been devoted to studying which she adored, and she could see very little away from this.

She pleased her parents.

She was young for marriage, even in those days when mere children were pledged each to the other. She asked that, for the moment she might return to her parents' home, complete her education there, and then return to the man whom she had married.

This young girl had experienced a most strange life. She had spent much of her childhood at court, with her cousins the Princess Elizabeth and the Prince of Wales. She had been extremely happy with Queen Katherine, the last of Henry's wives, and appalled when she had died in giving birth to her daughter. This meant that the child Jane, was returned to her parents.

She had by this time been bandied about in the most strange manner, first at home, then with the King's family, and later when His Grace died, to the Queen's Dower Palace where Katherine Parr had guarded her, cared for her, and had brought her up.

However, she was facing the astute brains of Seymour, and he knew what he was doing. In returning the child to her own people, he realized that perhaps he had made a bad mistake. Within ten days of his wife's death, and the whole world believed that he had had a hand in this, he was writing to Lord Dorset about the matter. He had suggested that the little girl returned to her people, over hastily, was what he said, and had changed his mind. Now he requested that he wished her to remain in this house, where she had been with the departed Queen. He himself had been in a state of horror over the unexpected death of his dear wife. He added to this letter

> *Unless your lordship expressed a mind to the contrary, or doubts the proof of my hearty affection towards you and my good-will towards her, I mind now, to* keep her, *until next I speak to your lordship.*

He had seen the poor child as the pawn in the game, and realized that his own mother would devote herself to the child as though she were her daughter, and he would be half her father himself.

Jane's father was not too sure of the effects of this. He wrote a most skilful letter begging that the girl's own mother should have charge of her, 'in these, her young years, wherein she now standeth either to make or mar (as the common saying is), the addressing of her mind to humility, soberness and obedience.'

It was a masterly letter. His wife wrote as well. They wrote with humility, not insisting as they had every right to do of course.

In the end it was agreed that the child should return to her rightful home which she did. Yet even when this was finally fixed, or so they thought, Seymour visited the house and had another long argument. Now everyone understood that the greatness of the argument abided with the fact that this child would be the King's bride, and one day the Queen of England.

The great man was determined to get his own way, and he recognized the fact that Jane's parents were at this moment not too well off. Money hath a strange method of unlocking all doors, even those of the heart and it happened now! Two thousand pounds was the price. In the face of so desirable a prize, the child's father wilted, and he let her stay where she was. The poor young girl had brought in a sum of money at a period of time when her father needed it.

Now in the charge of this unscrupulous man, she studied with her tutors and masters, had little time for amusement, and said that all her pleasure lay in the books that she read, and the studies which so absorbed her.

The country knew little of her. She was a princess—no more. Nobody cared for Seymour, neither did they trust him, how could they? An air of mystery lay about the death of his lady wife, in childbed, and the small daughter, as well. The man was well able to live down the sharp chatter of gossip. He was not afraid.

What he was aiming at, was to marry Jane to the King, and he felt almost sure that there would be no children of the marriage. The husband would be too sick, the wife very young! He himself would seek the Princess Elizabeth as his wife.

In those days marriage was merely a state of living which gave a man fuller rights, and, if the wife were rich, a larger income. When Edward the Sixth died, and anybody could realize that he would not live too long, his wife and the child Jane would retire from the world into one of those secret palaces which the eighth Henry had dotted about the country, and then he himself would come to the throne with the Princess Elizabeth, then Queen Elizabeth, as his wife.

This, he told himself, is all to the good.

* * *

The maxim that the best laid schemes of mice and men go oft astray has never outgrown its truth. The idea was good, and the one who would most benefit from it would be the man himself. But he had met a stern mistress in the child, Elizabeth, who was her father's own daughter. She was not prepared to wed anybody.

Now Seymour was discussed in the inns and alleyways of the city. People had seen behind that handsome face of his, and the polished good manners, and they recognized that he was *all* for himself! He tried to tie Elizabeth to him, and she maintained that she would do nothing.

'When the time comes to pass,' said Elizabeth, 'then I will do as God shall put into my mind.'

No more.

At this moment the whole country awaited the next move. Without a doubt the unwed King was rapidly dying. He was also, too young as yet for marriage. The Princess Mary lived quietly on, almost a recluse, and in silence, and the fear was that in her stern hands there lay the answer to the entire problem. Elizabeth would fall in with none of their ideas, but she committed herself to God and her studies. Nothing would change her.

She was, of course, extremely unpliable when it came to argument, and there was much of her father in her. She would have thought that Seymour was not getting far! He waited, but time was running out.

More difficult was the health of the poor young King! He had suffered what proved to be his worst relapse, and now lay sick unto death. Time was on the move. Jane's father found that his daughter was growing older, she was now fifteen, and it was time that she should be wed.

'This cannot continue for ever,' he maintained.

Seymour demurred. This was not the hour in which to raise the point, for the King was seriously ill and of course all knew that *he* should be the husband selected. When His Grace recovered slightly, he asked to see his coz, and the Lady Jane was brought to him.

The girl entered the putridly stinking sickroom which would in the end be this young man's death chamber, as she knew. She curtseyed low. She was horrified when she found that she could hardly recognize the skeleton of what had once been her cousin and who now lay there. He had always had the Tudor skin, bright as his father's, but now it was pale grey in colour, the grey of half dead autumn ditches in which the brightness of summer time leaves, and gay flowers rot and die.

Nurse Penn, ever loyal to her duty, sat beside him, applying fresh cool bandages to his brow, and pathetic eyes sought Jane's. But they were the eyes of an old man who sees the unwanted visitor close to his own bedside, and would if he could have done, have writhed from him.

Now he had not the strength left.

When he saw the girl whom he truly loved he greeted her with very real affection.

'Jane? My own dear coz! My sweet Jane,' he said, and then, 'this last has been the worst attack that I have ever had, and death will not hurry himself. When living is so terrible as it is to me, what man in the world would ever ask to live?'

'I weep for Your Grace.'

He choked then, for he was, as she knew, close to tears himself, yet somehow he swallowed them down and contrived to speak again.

'My sweet Jane! If God had willed it differently, and I had not inherited from my forebears, this foul cross, which too many of us are forced to bear, things could have been so different, and—for me—so happy! But I must die, already I see the stranger standing in the doorway of my life, and his hands are beckoning to me.' He put out his own hand which had grown so transparent, that she believed she could actually see the bones there. The hand was now yellowish, and so thin that it could have been made of tulle.

'I would have been enchanted, Sire, for I have always loved your most Royal Highness,' she said, and then she kissed him with very real affection.

He panted as he talked to her, she knew it was tiring him horribly, but what could she do? He said tenderly, 'You and I were meant for one another, my own sweeting. My Jane!'

She whispered, 'I love you, Sire.'

'My Jane! My sweet Jane,' he said.

'I weep for Your Grace,' and there was a deep sweet sympathy in her tone, for it was true. King or no King, lover or no lover, he was the boy she had known all her life, and, he *had* loved. She wanted him. In that tremulous voice of his he said, 'If God had willed it differently I could have asked you to share my throne and my crown. I could have made you my Queen of England, remaining faithful to you all my life. You would have been my wife and the mother of my sons.'

'I would have thanked God daily for my happiness, and my good fortune, Sire,' she said, and kissed him with a very real affection.

'I know.' He choked down the tears which he felt might disgrace him. 'We were made for one another, you and I,' and then, as he said it, the hacking cough took possession of him again, and raged. She waited until he had done with it. Then he spoke again. 'I was born to be the King of England, and I have executed my duty as I believe my father would have asked of me.'

'You have indeed, Sire.'

'The new prayer book is passed, and I have dedicated my failing strength to it. It is most urgent for the future of the English people.' He coughed again, recovered himself, and then, but more weakly, resumed the conversation which he felt so vital to him. 'I fear much that my sister Mary will make severe trouble, for she could easily do this. Poor Mary! She has much to learn and has endured too great sadnesses in her own life. Her fondness for her mother did, in the end, embitter her. But she was good to that mother of mine, I know, for many have told me how kind she was. My birth deprived me of a mother, I know t-that. Mary hel-ped me then.'

He said it sadly, and looking at him, Jane saw how desperately ill he looked. The King is dying, she thought, and instantly, with some horror, Long Live the Queen! If Mary became the Queen, what would happen now, to all those who, following the teaching of the late King, had turned to the Protestant Church? She did not dare think of it! The fires would be lit again at Tyburn, and the axe would fall at The Tower.

'Is there nothing we could do to put this straight?' she asked.

He told her that he had already despatched his emissaries to speak with the Princess Mary, and ask her to adopt a more reasonable attitude towards the new Church, but she had stayed stoical. She was a rock of iron he knew, and she had said that nothing would change her.

'She would mow down the faithful Protestants,' he said, and his voice was sad.

'I know.'

'I love Elizabeth,' he told her, 'and she would be a great queen and do well, but if I appointed her to follow me, then Mary would arm the entire world to fight her. The smell of smoke at Tyburn would be bitter, the axe at The Tower and the torture racks would be working overtime. It would be the era of destruction, and I want peace, and quiet good ruling, and the end of all this torture and cruelty.'

'You mean there is nothing we can do.'

'Nothing.'

Another fit of violent coughing almost paralysed him, but he recovered again. He had been so weakened by it that she could hardly understand the words that he said, and she felt that he was too weak and ill to accept this burden. The load was too great for him to carry. When he had recovered a little he spoke again.

'It would seem that whomsoever I do select, will be wrong,' he said, 'and that to establish the Church about which my good father had such faith, is already dangerous. There is none I can set on the throne to come after me and defend me. What next?'

'I am sure that you will arrive at the right conclusion, Edward my dearest,' she told him.

The old nurse signalled from behind the bed, that he was tiring badly, and must not do more! The girl rose and curtseyed.

'When next we meet, dear Edward, I do pray that you are better,' she said.

He shook his head. 'When we meet again it will be in Heaven, not on earth any more,' he told her, and the coughing began yet once more.

She made her *adieux*.

* * *

Of course the shadow in the background, carefully watching every step that was taken was Northumberland. He was the man who planned ahead, and now he had arrangements for his fourth son and his favourite, Guildford Dudley. He believed, perhaps erroneously, that the Princess Mary had been absent from the Court too long, and there must be some appearances made, she must be re-introduced into their midst, if she was to keep her place as the future Queen. He was wrong in this. He would have done better to leave things as they were, but he was not that sort of man.

The Princess Elizabeth was too young to think of as a bride for his son, to help him re-establish another generation who could pull the strings at court, and so re-establish the family for the lives to come. But the Princess was autocratic. She wanted her own way as much as he did, and when two of a kind meet together, there is often a difficulty.

The King would die unwed. Then Mary would make a bid for the throne, and lose. He doubted if the Princess Elizabeth would raise any opposition, and the third person due for the crown was Lady Jane Grey. If he could marry his son to the girl *now*, then in the future he would have every right that he could wish, and Dudley would go with her to Westminster

Abbey as her consort.

The marriage of the girl Jane, and his fourth son was the most demanding choice of the moment. It was the first urgency! They knew one another and were not averse. Jane was an obedient girl, and his son was as avaricious as his father was, not to want a seat beside the crowned head of the country.

Jane was approached by her mother, under Northumberland's insistency and the thought of having her own daughter as the future Queen of England, inspired the good lady much. She tried to talk the girl round, insisting that obedience was one of the first demands of God. At first she argued, then she became more gentle. Dudley was a good-looking man, slightly older than was Jane, but gay with it. She had to admit that, when she met him, he enchanted her, and always would. Finally Jane consented to the union.

Her love was ever for the dying King, but he could not wed, and this was true! She was not averse to this amiable young man, always beautifully dressed, and giving her the most handsome gifts so that her friends told her how fortunate she was. He was both eloquent and amusing, and he made love with the polished gallantry of the period. It was the era of lovers.

It is unlikely that this girl ever consulted her own desires and hopes for the future, but she wished to obey her father and mother, sure that this was right for her to do. She would wed this lover, bestowed on her by diplomacy, and she promised it.

Fair-headed, she had grey-blue eyes. Her nose was a little long, and she had an extremely short upper lip, said to be a notable beauty. She did not follow the fancy of the all-plucked eyebrows of that date when women discarded brows.

When the news started going the rounds (as of course it did), some said that the happy pair looked like children, and indeed the girl did.

The marriage was a triple one, with an enormous feast to follow it. The girl looked lovely but was very pale, the young man obviously distressed in some way, and nervous about that. All the arrangements had been hurried up, so that it was ill-planned, but the worsening condition of the boy King, made urgency vital to them.

There were to be the three marriages in one. To the general public the announcement which came quite suddenly, was a surprise. None had heard a rumour of them. Three brides went to the altar with three hand-picked husbands-to-be, and one of them would be a Queen, if only for the briefest possible time. There were rejoicings, and singing, and all those games and symbols of love, and goodwill, which were believed to be vital to a marriage of this kind.

But that night the bride told her young

husband that, at the mere fifteen years of age which she was, she had no wish to become his wife, but would ask consideration. She desired above all things to return to her mother's house, of which she was deeply fond, and there to be permitted to continue her studies for a few more months, and to come back to him and the fuller order of marriage, when she was older.

History gives no word of what happened. The only account that can be found is that both of them were considerably fatigued by the festivities, the dancing and the ceremonials, and had come to the agreement to sleep apart. In fact, the little girl Jane returned with her mother to her childhood home that very next day.

Here she continued her studies and thought little more of her marriage, or of the man who was, in the eyes of God and the law, her husband! The Princesses Mary and Elizabeth had completely ignored the proceedings, though of course they were both vigorously aware of them and the plans which lay behind them. Possibly there was no action that they could take, even if they had wished to do so, and one imagines that the relations *did* wish this. They waited.

The boy King had made a will, and in this will he had acted on the advice of his tutors, and his masters. He had been persuaded to leave his crown away from his two half-sisters, jumping over them to the third candidate on the roll, and this was Jane! He knew that he could trust her wisdom, and her generosity of purpose, also her truthfulness and her devotion to duty. He privately feared for the religion into which his father had been born, and preferred the Protestant faith which his father had founded as being the more lenient to his strange habits, and now with death approaching, the boy wished above all other things, to establish the faith more firmly.

He must have done this before her marriage, for in the actual wording, he alludes to her as the Lady Jane *Grey*, which would not have been her name when she was espoused to Guildford Dudley.

Now he himself was coming to the end of the road.

He clung to life, possibly entirely owing to the goodness of his kind old nurse, and her devotion. He clung on to something one could not describe as living, though it was not actually dying, until the summer of 1553. None seem to have been there when he died, certainly the Lady Jane was absent, the Princess Elizabeth at Hatfield, and the Princess Mary at Hunsdon. He died in the arms of the old nurse, who possibly had been the best friend this poor lad had ever had. He lay apparently unconscious yet at times it was seen that his pale lips moved in prayer for the country which had been left to him. Possibly he knew, by some strange intuition that before this country came to the calm waters of the Elizabethan reign, horror would be. He said that he was faint, and they brought him the cold water for which he had asked.

On the following day it was announced that the last of the Tudor Kings had gone to his fathers.

★ ★ ★

Instantly there was disturbance everywhere. There was no communication from either of the late King's sisters. Jane was told what had happened and she wept continuously as she heard the church bells starting to toll their dismal reminder that a King lay dead. The shops shut up, and all curtains were drawn so that the eternal twilight of death entered the homes of the people.

In the city there was chatter and gossip. The brothels saw better days coming, unless of course, Princess Mary won the day, then it would be death for far too many. What about that little scarecrow, scraggy Elizabeth? they asked. About her they knew little for nobody had been really interested in the late King's two sisters.

The few who 'thought of little Jane', did so casually, unaware of the fact that her people had awaited this moment to ensure their own promotion to better positions. She had been the quiet princess, who loved her lesson books, and working with them, even after she herself was married to young Dudley.

'The King is dead, Long Live the King—or Queen. But which King—or Queen?' There were of course four girls, all heirs to this throne, when the hour came, and if one analysed the problem properly, not one had precedence over the other. Which of the others would it be? The first two had been declared to be illegitimate, both Mary, a King and royal princess's daughter, and Elizabeth the same king's daughter, but her mother merely a lady of the court. Did the order of illegitimacy stand firm? There seemed to be no certainty of this, or uncertainty either. Mary was unpopular, save with the Catholics who would have done anything to get her back on the throne, and the 'rightful' Church reinstated. But even the Catholics themselves did not like her as a woman.

There was strong feeling about the Princess Elizabeth, a quiet student at the time being, and clever it was said. But she would support the Church which her father had insisted on, and which now was the supreme Church under her brother's government. The country had always disliked Elizabeth for the pain and suffering and the outrageous manner in which her mother had treated the poor Spanish princess, who had reigned in Katherine's place, with Henry.

Next came Lady Jane Grey, and the French Queen, both unknown quantities, the first girl studious, said to be most accomplished; the Scottish girl (married in France) was said to be flirtatious, very beautiful and attractive, but not too trustworthy.

Quite suddenly, Jane's father-in-law sent for her, in the nature of a royal command. He stated that she must come, and said that her cousin, the suffering young King, had died during the night, and that he had appointed her as his heir to the throne. When she came to the great house, she was ushered into the great salon where he awaited her, approaching her, and kissing hands.

'I kiss the hand of the Queen of England,' was what he said, and she stared at him, dismayed.

At first she was horrified, and could not believe that any of this was true. If Edward had appointed her as his heiress, surely he would have told her this, and he had said nothing about it at all. They had talked of the next King or Queen, of course, but mainly it had been with his keen determination at whatever cost, to keep the Princess Mary from stepping into the niche. 'If she reigns, I know instinctively that England will run with blood, the blood of good men and true,' was what he said.

It was probably true!

'What—what do I do now?' she asked him.

'You return home, and await instructions, Madam.'

'What if I ... I do not desire to become Queen? I am sure that Elizabeth would do better than I ever could.'

'If the Princess Elizabeth now stepped into the gap, there would be war between the two sisters! The last thing that the country desires.'

Possibly Jane knew that this was true! War happened so easily, and was so cruel. It would have been the last thing that poor Edward would have wished, and now he lay in the Abbey Church, awaiting burial. He had had so little from life, this boy on whom the faith of hundreds had been staked, and all that was over, for ever!

When Jane returned home she immediately received another message. A boat waited her and she was to depart for Syon House in Isleworth. She had a deep affection for this sweet place, where that poor child Queen Kathryn Howard had been imprisoned for months. How that poor girl must have prayed for her pardon and release but knew goodness was unlikely from a man like Henry.

This house and grounds had been granted to Northumberland who owned it, and now sent the urgent message that it was to this great house that the Lady Jane should be escorted, there to wait for further instructions.

She wished to stay in London, even if she loved Syon, but she went obediently, because this was expected of her, and she was dutiful by nature. She was rowed down to Syon, on a calmly restful day, when there came the pleasant scent of water, and the fat yellow lilies like golden curls floated a'top it, with great green saucers of leaves. It was a happy trip for her.

She had no idea that already an urgent message had been dispatched to the Princess Mary, telling her that the King was dying and entreating her to come to be with him in his last hours. The Princess must have been suspicious of this, and she would not go. Had she done so, fate would have changed life. But she *suspected* Northumberland!

It is true that she did start the journey from Hunsden, but she got very little of the way, for, when she reached Hoddesden, she was told that the King was dead, he had in fact, been dead when the first command had come to her, and the second message warned her that, whatever else she did, she must not place herself in the hands of his enemies.

Instantly she fled.

It was the only thing that she could do, and she turned north, believing at that moment that this would be the safest place for her to go. It is highly probable that, in this, she was right! For the moment Northumberland was king of the situation, and everything was going as he wished; how easy it would be to make the wrong move! These were vital hours, and he recognized this.

It was at Syon House that Jane learnt that she was the Queen of England, and must prepare to accept the crown which her cousin had left to her. His will had set aside the two princesses of the blood royal, and the heritage was handed to Lady Jane Grey, as his nearest of kin.

The girl when she heard sighed heavily.

'Too much happens too speedily,' was what she said.

Her mother was with her, to comfort and help her, and with her the Duchess of Northumberland. Between them they tried to explain what had happened, and how she was within her rights. She was not setting herself queen, when the two other girls had a right to it, it was *hers*!

The earls prostrated themselves, and swore her as being their rightful queen, vowing that, if called upon, they would shed blood and give up their lives, to honour her graciousness, and her goodness.

In this hour the very young and amazed girl had no idea what she could do about it nor if she was doing right or wrong. She turned to God and prayed.

'God give me grace, and power to praise His glory and dedicate myself to His service,' she said, 'and ever for the good of this, which is His brave realm.'

She saw in her dreams a noble land going forth to better things, and prayed that her virtue and her goodness would do good and help those who trusted her as their Queen.

So far everything was going the way that Northumberland had anticipated, and he must have been well pleased with the action that he had taken. The King was dead, and he himself had in his will appointed his successor. None could blame any other person for this, and none would lose their head on that account. Northumberland told Jane that it was her cousin who had arranged everything and that, as soon as the proper arrangements could be made, she would return to London, to The Tower (the part of the building which was known as being a palace, and where those who awaited their crowning spent the time previous to that crowning).

Northumberland would have got her there immediately but she demurred. She wept bitterly for the loss of the cousin whom she had loved dearly, she was unnerved by the fact that she *was* the Queen, and had not yet recovered from the shock.

Northumberland had made all his plans carefully, and as he handled them he recognized the danger attached to them. He believed that he was doing well, for he had received the news that the Princess Mary had started for London, believing her brother to be still alive, but dying (he himself had had this message despatched to her) and that now she had turned back again. That was all to the good, but now the City had to receive the girl, and aver that they agreed to her right to the throne. London must be convinced that Jane was the proper heiress, then they could move ahead. Actually, before the young girl even knew that she was Queen, the Lord Mayor with six aldermen and some of the city merchants had been secretly informed of the King's death.

Lady Jane Grey was entirely ignorant of what was going on behind her back! She had been whisked off to Syon, her mother with her, and they had argued a few moments quite bitterly. The girl wanted explanations, her mother was not prepared to give them. The nobles had however accepted her as being their Queen, and she was their Queen. From Northumberland's point of view it looked as if it could not go wrong.

Lady Jane Grey wrote pitifully of her cousin for whom she had cared deeply.

I lamented much the death of so noble a prince; and at the same time turn to God, humbly praying and beseeching Him that, if what was given me in truth, and legitimately mine, He would grant me grace and power to govern to His glory and service, and for the good of this realm.

Poor little girl! She had been shuffled into the most dreadful alleyway from which there was no escape, but for the time being, she believed what she was told and did not shrink from those in authority over her.

It was on the tenth of July that Jane was brought according to the usual custom which was right and proper, of all kings who spent the night before their crowning in the Palace of The Tower. She was received at the gate by Northumberland himself, and an enormous crowd had assembled to watch the ceremony in which she formally accepted the keys. The crowd stared. There was the strange feeling of general discomfort in the air. None disliked the brave young girl, she was popular, but somehow they had never thought of her coming here to await her crowning. There were two other princesses, both daughters of the old king, and surely they came first? The Roman Catholics thought of this as being their most exquisite moment for success; the Protestants were afraid!

She was taken to her rooms, the floor spread with sweet-smelling fresh straw for the occasion, and the Marquis of Windsor, who was the Treasurer, brought the crown jewels for her to see, and with them the actual crown of England itself.

He asked her to try on the crown for size, but this she refused to do! She had some vague occult warning that it would be wrong. She made excuses, and in the end, he accepted these. She dare not have felt the crown on her brow, yet did not know why it was that she was so nervous about it, so apprehensive, and strangely unhappy.

There came next another problem, which she faced calmly, but with some inner apprehension. It was proposed to her that her husband, young Guildford Dudley, would wish to be crowned with his wife, and instantly she realized this would never do! She was Tudor on her mother's side, and *had* the right, but Dudley had no royal relations of this kind. Instantly, she changed her attitude. She was no longer the smiling happy girl, prepared to accept everything that was suggested to her. There were certain rules and relations which she must *not* accept.

The person who was most surprised was Guildford himself. It had to be explained to him, and he was amazed at this young girl's knowledge and her proficiency as she faced him in the panelled room.

'None of this is easy,' she said, 'and you must recognize that the part which I have to play, is particularly difficult.'

'But why? Surely you always realized that you might be Queen, if the two daughters of the late King were set aside?'

Rather pitifully, she said, 'I . . . I am not at all

sure that they *should* be set aside.'

Perhaps if she had been in love with this young man she would not have seen through him as she did. His marriage had been for self-betterment. Northumberland had told him that it could mean the throne of England, shared with his wife, but any wise husband knew how to keep his wife reined-in and make himself felt.

Guildford was furious. In the end it was pointed out to him that he could only be made King by Act of Parliament, and this was something which nobody intended to do on his behalf.

'I am prepared to make him a Duke,' the new young Queen said to her uncles, 'but no more! I would never agree to his being made a King.'

This was the first time that she had asserted herself, and she stuck by it. She was approached both by her husband and his mother, who thought that she was behaving very badly indeed.

'I have my own principles,' she said quietly, 'and I must do what I believe to be for the good of all; in this I am not prepared to be swayed by other influence. I have my duty to perform, and I shall perform it.'

She could believe that she was the Queen. She sought time to decide what was proper for the future, but never seemed to have a single moment for herself. In some way she was glad that she had come to the Palace of The Tower, for this did not seem to be threatening. Her rooms were nice, there were fresh flowers, and that comfortably sweet scent of fresh straw. So far there was a mystery about the death of the King, and it was not actually announced until the tenth day of the month, and then proclaimed.

> *After seven o'clock at night, there was made a proclamation in Cheap, by three heralds and one trumpet ... for Jane, the Duke of Suffolk's daughter ... to be Queen of England.*

It was tragic that this announcement should be greeted by a silent calm, none made a sound. One would have anticipated cheering, but the London populace were in a state of complete bewilderment, and so were others. Had it been the Princess Mary, or even Princess Elizabeth they could have understood it, but not this.
Perhaps the poor young girl most concerned, had already sensed that it was going wrong for her. The young King was dead, his successor had been appointed and was here installed in the Palace of The Tower of London. She was bemused.
One had to remember that nothing was yet threatening, but all the people were awaiting the crowning, and her coming here the night before her coronation, to sleep as was the duty and the practice of those times, in this the palace side of

the great massive building, and to ride forth from there through the city to Westminster for their coronation on the next day.

The girl had seen the jewels and the crown. She sat there now alone, as she had asked, and her ladies had withdrawn. In her own personal diary, she wrote.

He did ask me to put the crown on my head, to try if it did fit me or not. I did refuse with many excuses, but he insisted that I should take it, and said that another would be made for my husband, which I did most certainly hear unwillingly, and with infinite grief and displeasure.

Perhaps for the first time she now realized that she was surrounded by those who would defeat her. She knew very little of the man who was said to be her husband, and nowhere is there any word which shows that she treated him with any especial affection, nor even that she loved him unduly. She had always been a good obedient girl, and she had done what she was told. Her marriage to Guildford Dudley had been part of the poor child's instructions.

The Duchess of Northumberland was furious that the girl had behaved this way, and she came indignantly to The Tower to say so. It did not matter to her if it was a period of time when there was suspense, extreme danger, and anxiety for the future. The angry duchess was indignant with her daughter-in-law and she said so.

'He should be a King, and you know it,' she said.

'I have no right to make him King, even if I am Queen.'

'You could create that right. It has been done before.'

'At the moment I have no wish to do anything which could offend, and therefore would not take liberties of this kind. I refuse to do it, for it is not right and I will not permit it.'

The older woman was furiously angry that the girl, even if she thought that she was the Queen, something she would never have been if Northumberland had not exerted his influence as he had done, should behave so rudely.

'You are behaving disgracefully, how dare you speak to me like this?'

'I have a perfect right to use my prerogative as Queen of England.'

For a second abashed, but never for very long, the older woman said, 'But you are also related by marriage to me, and I will not see you behave so wrongly as to turn on *me*! You do not know how to behave.'

'That is untrue.'

The girl would have done anything to stay the argument, but did not stand a chance with this indignant woman. She was overcome by the thought of having the Queen of England in her family, even if only as an in-law. She raged a while, the girl watching her fearless and gone dead quiet. At last she terminated it.

Arguing like this will help neither of us, the least that we can do is to behave according to our duty, and not be perverse each with the other.'

'You are new to Queenship,' flashed the indignant Lady Northumberland.

'It is a degree to which you and your own family will never come,' defied the girl.

They argued and it ended, but that night poor Jane prayed, 'Oh God, help your daughter for pity, help her.' She lay there thinking about the future, wondering what lay ahead of her, and what she ought to do then she broke down, into violent weeping, but later conquered the tears, feeling better for them. A strange new world had opened itself and engulfed her. Half of her had fear, the other half believed that she would be guided, and lead as she had so far in her life been led.

She slept but little that night.

★   ★   ★

In the entire country there was a general feeling of intense dismay over the death of the young King. He had made a mark on the nation, this lad, who had wished all men well, and whose one desire had been to establish the Church of England, and make it secure. He had undoubtedly, in the last years of his life, worked himself to death over the Common Prayer Book, which he had felt was his life's mission! Now he lay awaiting burial in Westminster Abbey with twenty-four sentries around him, keeping guard over that wretchedly emaciated body of his, for it had gone completely to skin and bones. None knew what would happen next. The Princess Mary was unpopular, save with the Catholic following who saw her as their leader to the re-installation of their Church in England. She had never had a likable personality, nor had she made much of a mark in the world.

Of her sister, the Princess Elizabeth (the only child of the much disliked Anne Boleyn who had behaved so badly to the unfortunate Katherine of Aragon), little was known, and there was possibly some feeling of dislike. Of the three children she was the most like her father, with her red hair, and penetrating eyes. As a child she had sparkled of course, but since she grew older little had been seen of her, and she had retired somewhat into the country. The young King had been devoted to her. She was the King's favourite sister, of course, but Princess Mary was a disagreeable girl, suffering from constant migrainous headaches which made her miserable and touchy.

The world had hardly heard of Lady Jane Grey, only that she had played with the others as a child, and that the late King had been fond of her, and had been going to marry her, save that his illness had increased so savagely that, by the time he was eleven years old his physicians gave up all thought of his ever reaching his majority.

The Scottish Mary was better known, even though when young, she had gone to France, and there had married the Dauphin, herself a mere child at the time.

But the thought of the two last claimants for the crown went by the board. It would undoubtedly be one of Henry's daughters, and whilst the Catholics urged that it could only be Mary, she *was* the first-born, and had the prior rights, the Protestants prayed for Elizabeth to stake her claim to the throne in supporting the Church of England.

Princess Mary was not the woman to bide her time, already she had taken action. Her spies were everywhere, and kept her well versed with the news, and she knew that she must act wisely.

On the July night which was the eve of the day when Jane was proclaimed as being the rightful Queen, Mary wrote an impassioned letter to the Council! She expressed her astonishment, and concern, that none had written to tell her that her brother was dead, nor had they proclaimed *her* as being the Queen of England in the proper manner!

It would seem, and all manner of stories were going the rounds, that they had proclaimed another of the royal princesses. Princess Mary had always had spies around her, and they brought the news to her. The King was dead, and the Marquess of Northampton accompanied by the Earl of Shrewsbury had ridden into London from Greenwich. Both went to The Tower of London.

They were there some time, and Princess Mary herself a very artful woman knew that whatever arrangements they had made would scarce be in her personal favour.

News was brought to her. She was dark with rage. This was not largely because she disliked poor Jane so much, but because she—and she *was* the rightful heiress to the crown—was being passed over.

'They would pass *me* by, and this they shall never do, for I will fight for my rights, and to the very last,' and she added proudly, 'I have the blood of Henry in me!'

There were other things which were noted, and news of them despatched by loyal Catholics to the one woman whose birth and rights lay with the throne. The great guns were hauled to the top of the White Tower, and mounted there. This was not usually done, but it indicated that there was apprehension from those who were in power that there might be some argument which could evoke gunfire, or some change of power, or some step which was not entirely within the conformation of justice.

Then the chatter began. The ale houses had rumours, and the brothels were full of talk. The Captain of the King's Guard announced to his bowmen that the King was dead, swore them to the Crown, and then told them a little more of the King's will.

Throughout the entire country there was this confusion of liking and disliking, connected with the Church of Rome. It was true that the old Monasteries had done good, but there had been all manner of atrocities, the hanging, and the burning of people, and the hard arm of the law, backed by the insistence of the indignant Church!

That had been the time when heads had rolled into the straw on Tower Hill, and there was that constant stench of burning at Tyburn on the New Oxford Road, and no one knew how long this would last. The monks had helped, they said, and blamed the religious code.

Edward the Sixth had reigned with calm peacefulness, he had been just, because he loathed torment, and massacre, and would have none of it whilst he lived. The people had trusted him. Now they looked in dismay each to the other, not sure what would happen and whom they might trust. They suspected Northumberland who was one of the nobles for ever pushing his way up in the world, and coming nearer and nearer to the throne. If Jane succeeded, and the story was being prattled round the alleyways, and the cockpits, that the crown had been left to her by the late King, and it would be Northumberland who would be ruling! Then Heaven only knew how shocking life could be! All men disliked him, and few had a good word to say for him.

The country was trained to seek a royal princess to come to the Stone of Scone, not what they termed the 'poor relation', as this could be, for obviously the heir was her Majesty Queen Mary, the sister of the King.

Nothing stifled the city chatter.

The whores laughed together. Whoever came to the throne would find it hard going! Neither of the princesses were married, and Mary was no beauty, getting on in years, for most princes sought a fair bride and one young with firm white flesh, and bright eyes. There would be little to attract them in the pock-marked, haggard woman, whose life had been already spent in suffering, and care for the mother whom she had adored.

It is extremely unlikely that, in this tense hour when her own fate and her life, or death, hung in the balance, that poor little Jane knew much of what was going on. Northumberland would have told her nothing, until he felt that the right moment had struck for it. She would not have suspected what was coming, even if the King had left her as his heiress, which as yet she did not know.

The Tower of London, palace or garrison had the most excellent methods of keeping its secrets closed, and told nothing. In the hour when England waited for the announcement, Northumberland waited until the first fuss died down, then was sure that everything would settle smoothly. He possibly believed that Mary had been half-forgotten, forgetting that, if she were pushed aside, none had overlooked the glory of the Church which she held so dear, and for which, in this hour, she stood as the woman who would bring it back to England. She had never been a personality who forgot different details. She had her watchful eye on everything, and the Church would have supported her in this.

If Northumberland thought that he was playing for safety he was wrong. He found that out later.

NINE

Pale death knocks with impartial foot at the cottages of the poor, and at the towers of kings.

Horace

THE Ambassadors overseas received news of the young King's death unofficially, before the despatches arrived, and none could be surprised at it. His demise had been long anticipated, but the amazing point was that no mention was made of his successor. Neither of his sisters had been appointed as Queen in his place, and there was no mention of his cousins Jane or Mary. It was not within the boundaries of the law to pass over the legal heir because of some strange report that she had been born out of wedlock, or some years after her birth pronounced a bastard. King Henry the Eighth had been a King with strange fancies, the world knew this, but his son had been a sincere young man, riddled by bad health, and doomed almost from infancy, never to reach man's estate. Now not unexpectedly he had died.

He would have been brought to Westminster Abbey, there to lie in state with a guard of soldiers about him. Had he mentioned his heir? He *had* done, but this for the moment was held a secret. The moment that suspicion was aroused it was a flame, which blown by the wind of chance, flickered in this direction, and the other, and the gossip began speeding its way.

It is of course a fact that Princess Mary recognized the fact that she, poor woman, stood in very grave danger! She suspected foul play. Nobody knew of the general dislike of her as a woman which adhered to her image, and which she could never tear aside.

She detested Northumberland, and knew that

he was for the moment, a mighty power in the country. The fact that no announcement had been made, as was usual, and with speed, told her that he was at the back of some strange scheme which she distrusted.

July the 9th was a Sunday, when one would expect nothing in the way of news, and no set movement to be made, but there was one detail which was noticed. The names of the late King's two sisters were omitted from the prayers. Instantly this set rise to all manner of stories.

The next detail which excited comment was on the Monday when it was discovered that the Council was not now at Greenwich, as was usual but had gone down to Syon House, the home of the Duke of Northumberland, and there at this time, was Jane.

She had come there suddenly summoned, not knowing why she was sent for. It was true that she had heard already that Edward had mentioned her as being his successor, and he had told her of doing this, so that it was no surprise to her. She was now sixteen, nearing seventeen, not wildly thrilled by what she had heard, in fact, rather the other way for she did not know what to do. At Syon, when she came there, she was fêted, and the Lords of the Council all knelt at her feet asking her to give her consent to accepting the crown which the late King had left to her.

She must have been at a loss, seeing all this

going on. Her parents too, who had been hard with her as a child, commandingly stern for ever ordering her about as they believed was the right way to bring up a child. Now they fawned upon her. Her mother, an irritable woman who had been extremely severe at times, smiled upon her, and flattered her so that the girl could not believe what was happening to her. Hailed already as a queen is hailed, and, though at first she did not believe what they said to her, towards the end of the evening, she came to the conclusion that it was true.

They would not have let her be until she was persuaded. They could prove the fact that her cousin had wished it, for he had told her so, and once had suggested that he could leave her the crown, possibly unaware of the fact that it was not his to leave to another.

'How can you all feed and wine so well when the King is dead?' she asked at last.

'All mourn the King,' her father told her, 'but we also fête the new Queen. You stand in his shoes. You go to the Stone of Scone to receive his crown.'

'But what about Mary and Elizabeth?'

He ignored the stupid question. 'The King himself commanded this, and we obey the dead King.'

She had to accept the truth.

She was now established in the palace side of The Tower, and overcome by a deadly and tormenting fear. It is true that she heard none of the gruesome sounds which The Tower had in good store. The screams of men dying on the rack, the horrors of torment. Pathetically, she said, 'I wish to God that my coz Edward were here and with me to guide me now, for I am sore a'feared.'

But now she was being carried along on the high tide of the plans others had made for her. She had no time to do what she desired, only to interview strange men brought to her for this, only to pray for the future, only to ask guidance!

London itself was agog with interest, and some of them with sheer dismay as to what was now going on. They had believed Queen Mary would come next, and the loyal Catholics were excited about this. Somehow, they had never even given the Lady Jane a second thought as coming to the throne. The King had had two sisters. They would inherit, as was right and proper, and this pronouncement about the Lady Jane as Queen, was one which astounded them. She was here in the palace, awaiting the arrangements for her crowning to go through and this horrified them.

Northumberland had found the situation far easier to manage, than he would have expected it to be. He was backed by merely three thousand fighting men, and he had also the right to the armour which was kept in The Tower of London, and which was a goodly display. But three thousand is not a big army. The new Queen now had but to be crowned.

He saw little danger ahead, the danger would have lain in the beginning, not to what was happening now, he thought.

A proclamation had declared the Ladies Mary and Elizabeth to be bastards, Jane was the heir! 'And foreasmuch as the said limitation of the Imperial crowns of this realm being limited, as is aforesaid to the said Lady Mary, and the said Lady Elizabeth, being illegitimate, the marriage between the late King Henry the Eighth and the Lady Anne, mother to the said Lady Elizabeth, being clearly undone by sentence, according to the word of God and the ecclesiastical laws. The Ladies Mary and Elizabeth are to all intents and purposes, divested of claim or challenge to the imperial crown, or any other honours, etc., appertaining thereto. . . .'

From the point of view of Northumberland all this was highly satisfactory, and it had gone off without a flaw. It could not have been better. What next?

What did happen next was amazing for most certainly one of the most uncharming princesses we have ever had, in our royal family, found that fate was on her side.

The royal Princess Mary was used to woe, to grief, and to disappointment, for she had suffered far too much in her life, and things having reached the stage that they had reached one might have thought that this was the final, and the most bitter pill of all for her to swallow.

However, she had a friend in Sir Harry Jermiah, a most loyal Catholic who proved to be her greatest ally. He had departed into the Norfolk and Suffolk boundaries, there looking for the men who would be prepared to fight for the lady whom he termed (and with a very large proportion of truth) to be 'the rightful queen'.

It had very recently been extremely bad weather, with strong gales blowing, and big seas coming in and breaking on the shores; as he approached Yarmouth itself, Sir Harry learnt that Northumberland had despatched this day six ships, with the idea of interception of any flight which might be attempted across the water to the Continent and an escape from what he called justice. Because the weather had been so shocking, that progress seemed to be impossible, these ships had taken shelter in the kinder waters of Yarmouth harbour, where they were now riding safely at anchor. On such small details as this is history made.

He rowed out to the six ships, and there he personally interviewed the captains, each in turn. He did this with the idea of determining where their loyalties lay. Were they Catholic or Protestant, for it was on this question that the real argument lay. What was the future of this country to be, the religion of their fathers, or the one which Henry the Eighth had started creating, and which his son had done his best to make safe for the future? Did their dreams for the time ahead, lie with the late King's young cousin (who was a Protestant), or with his half-sister, the eldest child of the late King's father, and as such had the right of precedence to the throne?

Sir Harry was no light of heart, no half measured diplomat who was beating about the bush, he was determined to get down to the bedrock of all this. How did these fighting men feel about the problem of which girl now proceeded to the throne of England, and where did the loyalties of the people actually lie?

Most of them knew nothing of young Lady Jane Grey, but knew of the Lady Mary, and more remotely of the Lady Elizabeth, but were biased against her mother.

It was of course, a distinctly tricky move for any man to take, but was this the moment to take the risk? All the same he did it.

There were now but ten whole days in which to get up a show-down, to call a halt to argument, and recapture the crown, or place it (far more firmly) on the head of the innocent young girl who was being at this very hour, sheltered in The Tower of London, prior to her coronation. He got the answer that he required. When Sir Harry returned to Framlingham afterwards, he brought with him the Captains and their ships' crews, even the guns taken from the ships.

It was a brilliant piece of work!

To encourage them all, Mary reviewed her troops herself and riding before them on a milk-white steed, conducted herself quite magnificently as she rode along their lines. Although she was very plain, and had nothing at all to recommend her, when it came to looks, she *had* inspiration. It was something to see a woman leading her troops and behaving as she did in that hour. Every inch a queen, and they *were* quite right in feeling that about her! She was also no longer young, and in those days people aged earlier; she was badly pitted by the smallpox, and her eyes had sunk back into her head, but at the same time the very sight of her inspired the men! So much so that her milk-white steed shied, and in the end, she had to finish her review on foot.

This did not worry her.

She had established the cause in which she believed so firmly, none could ever doubt that. She was the rightful heir to the throne, and prepared, for the sake of her faith, to do everything that she could to establish this. More and more men came to fight for her, it was the old story of men fighting for a weak woman, which has for ever had sentimental appeal. None of them would have thought of the very young girl sleeping that night in The Tower of London, a little afraid of where she found herself, and the responsibilities which had been thrust so violently upon her. She had not thought of death, of course. She was right in feeling that she had done nothing wrong, and she trusted her advisers.

She was not to know at this very hour, the sight of her cousin on a milk-white steed had perhaps swayed the balance out of Jane's reach for ever. Nobody suspected this could happen.

The general unpopularity of the Princess Mary was well known, and none could for a single second have imagined that the wind of chance would change its course. But this was exactly what was happening, and the difficulty that made it worse was that it was all taking place so quickly; that those in power in London could not catch up with it! They were content and happier than they had been so far, believing that their cause was now established, and that they were ready for the coronation.

None were prepared for a rising.

Actually, whilst all this was going on, the rumour was in the bawdy houses, and the beer shops, that the Lord Warden of the Cinque Ports, and the Earl of Pembroke were both of them staying in the Tower and only waiting for the opportunity to slip out unseen to some private appointment with friends in London and cause fresh mischief for the young girl who lay awake wondering what next.

Evil was everywhere!

One has to remember that, for many years now, the plight of this country and the future of the crown (in which direction would it go, and who would eventually lay it fast) had been a topic of general debate. Since Henry had died, it had been apparent that his son would not succeed him for long. The boy's inherited condition had altered for the worse, when he was but nine years of age, and undoubtedly there would be trouble when he died. He *had* died and everything was shaping for a halt.

How much did the poor girl Jane know of what was going on around her? Very little, quite obviously, for she would have been far too bewildered by events, to give them a shape, or a name. None would have done anything to alarm her, even with goodwill, for that would have been too dangerous.

She was for the moment, in residence on the palace side of The Tower of London, but alas, it is but a short step from that very comfortable surround to another, which is not so happy! There, there is no fresh straw, no garlands, and no flowers. The stench of death is eternally within those ghastly cells, where men have died, have been murdered, and have rotted out what is left of their lives.

Of course, she did not know this, nor would she hear the grim noises when the scourge and the rack were on duty. Whilst she was in residence, it would be seen that no man in agony screamed himself to death, nor were criminal bodies kicked into the Thames to rot, as it passed by.

England was waiting for some stupendous event to happen and shape the future, and they were very close to one of the most stupendous tragedies that we have ever had.

Which Queen was it going to be? Mary, born to the throne without a doubt, or Jane, who had *not* been born to it?

Which indeed?

★   ★   ★

It was on the amiable evening of July the 16th, though still of course broad daylight, when the gates were shut, and the keys taken to Queen Jane, it was discovered that one of the most artful of the prisoners was missing from his cell.

It was the old Marquis of Winchester, who was not there! He had been the Treasurer, an ardent Catholic, and although he had not advertised it glibly (for that could have lost him his job) a supporter of Mary ever since her birth. He had been brought to The Tower from his pretentious house in London, but now there transpired serious news. The man who was commissioned to control the Royal Mint, had suddenly disappeared, and the news was that at this very moment, he was riding as hard as he could go to Princess Mary, and the army she was reputed to be mustering.

As yet it was mostly gossip, built on whispers suggesting all sorts of terrible events, more than fact. But was there fact behind the gossip? Was it true that Mary was on her way towards the city, where she would demand her crown? There was actual peril here in The Tower of London itself, for the country disliked Northumberland and was against him. It is possible that nobody thought for a single moment of the unfortunate girl imprisoned there (for that was what it was) awaiting her crowning. By July the 18th, pandemonium ensued!

Nobody knew quite where Northumberland was, nor how much poor Jane knew of the events that were happening. Possibly very little.

The body of the skeleton young King lay embalmed in the Abbey, awaiting the final ceremonies, but no great crowd filed past his lying-in-state, for the trend of other events was occupying most, and the anxiety as to what could happen next and where all this was leading them.

Jane still accepted the homage of a queen, and said little. Next day Guildford Dudley arrived there, and went immediately to his wife. He was dressed magnificently; he was by nature a conceited man and was assured that these circumstances which led to his wife's crowning would ultimately make him a King.

'You *are* a future King,' his father had told him, and it is possible that he had convinced himself that this was true.

Jane received him. One must remember that, although they had been married some time, she was still a virgin, which Northumberland had guessed, and he wanted to hurry things. He had sent for his son, and asked him to The Tower, claim her as his wife (which she was) for, as he added with truth 'England will expect a Prince of Wales of you.'

One of his wife's ladies led him to her room, and admitted him, and Jane turned to greet him. He knew instantly that she had changed. This was not the small child with whom he had played so gaily. She wore a magnificent dress, stood calmly there, and surveyed him with eyes which did not recognize him as a lover, but more as a friend.

Dudley prided himself that he was a man who could sweep any woman off her feet (and *had* done quite frequently) but he saw something about this young girl now, which he admitted he found difficult to understand, if not impossible! She was already a Queen in spirit. If his father had insisted that the marriage must be made tonight, the young man knew that it would not be easy. A river far wider than the Thames had stretched itself before him.

'Madam ... my wife ...?' he said, with

courtly dignity.

'Good evening, Sir,' and she held out her hand to be kissed.

'We live in strange times, Madam,' he said as he kissed it. As he came here, he had realized that the City of London was worried. There were those most unpromising small crowds at street corners, and all manner of people discussing the appointment of this new girl as Queen. Little was known of her; she had just been another lady of the Court, but the princesses all the world chattered about were Mary and Elizabeth.

In horror he asked himself what would they do if the Catholics rose, and brought Mary to London? He knew sufficient of that lady to be sure that she would never make that journey, unless she were sure of the end to it. She should have been arrested at the same time that Jane was brought to The Tower. He had said so, to his father, and there had ensued one of those horrifying scenes, for which Northumberland was famous. His father had only been a man of crafty design, who sought everything that life could give him, and a shade more for good fortune. In putting Jane here, he could quite easily have destroyed them all, he told himself.

He kissed her hand, and then her mouth. She drew back a little dismayed. 'None told me you were coming here, my Lord.'

'You are my wife. My place is by your side.'

She said, 'For the moment, Sir, great events are taking place and much has to be done. You have come to help me?'

'I love my wife, and have come to claim her as my wife,' and he bowed courteously.

But within this hour, he had realized how changed she was, more Queen than wife, more stranger than someone with whom he had danced and sang. What had happened? Under it all, the girl was desperately concerned, for somehow she felt in the atmosphere of The Tower something that she did not and could not understand. It had all happened so suddenly, and she had been brought here almost against her will, forced into queenship, made to dress herself as a queen, and wave to the crowd, and all the time, deep down in her heart, this strange little horror, which was irremovable.

She has gone mad, he told himself. Power has gone to her head, and because he was furious (he had had a merry night, but a few hours back and had not yet entirely recovered from the aftermath of it). He said, 'England demands sons of its Queens, and sons do not come through talking. Nor are they born of kisses.'

She looked at him almost as if she did not see him. Her eyes were sad, he wished that he did not feel sorry for her, but this he did.

She said, 'I am concerned tonight.'

'Too much has happened.'

'And too soon.' She said quickly, 'I wish I

could see my cousins, Mary and Elizabeth. Is there news of them?'

'None, Madam.'

'You could not ... you could not enquire...?'

'How could I hope to get news? Too many stories are being told.'

'What do they say?'

'Some that Mary is trying to raise an army.'

'Oh no, not that,' and she flushed with anxiety. 'This has been pushed through too fast! That is the trouble. Now what? Where do we go?'

'To the Abbey for your crowning,' he said.

'But am I the rightful Queen?'

Horrified that she should, for a single moment, think that she was not, he said. 'You would not be here spending the necessary time which is demanded in the palace of The Tower, to come forth for your crowning, if not the rightful Queen.'

'I am not sure.' She put her hand to her head, which was aching sadly. 'I am sure of nothing, and do not know what to do.' Then, 'Leave me Dudley, for now. I would pray for directions from God, for He alone can direct me. *Leave me.*'

He backed from the room through the sweet-smelling fresh straw brought here from the country this very morning. He was furiously angry with her for some things, for he *was* his father's own son, and wanted every glory, that the world could give him, without paying the sum that the world thought the action required.

They were giving him shelter in the palace, and he saw pleasant rooms prepared, and every comfort made ready for him. There was no sound of the tortures and the grass was green beneath his window. Tonight the accession of the new Queen would be announced, he knew; she was preparing for it now. Once the announcement was made, it would be difficult to go back on it!

It happened between five and six in the evening of that day. It had been sultry, almost like thunder riding up against the wind. The event took place as it had always done for other kings, with heralds and trumpeters, who announced the accession formally. But they had not reckoned on difficulties. These were unusual at a proclamation of this kind. Before the heralds got further than St. Paul's churchyard, people had heard that it was coming, and had formed barriers to block the way for them. It was almost a war here in the city.

The heralds came nearer, forcing the way, and now suddenly someone shrieked the words. 'God save Queen Mary', and instantly others took up the cry, screaming out, 'God save Queen Mary' all the time that the proclamation was being read, so that not a man heard a word of it.

It seems almost unbelievable that a woman, who was so unpopular for her cruelty, her ill looks and lack of graciousness, could have accumulated so large a crowd! Of course, her accession was right and proper; she *was* the heir, and even if this was the last time that she would ever be popular again, Mary *was* the rightful Queen.

She had never been liked, some had hated her for the evil that she did, yet suddenly, at this hour, when the other girl, one who was entirely harmless, kind and gentle, and had little idea of what was really going on, had been brought to the palace of The Tower to await her crowning. Perhaps the antipathy was not for herself, but for that faith which she represented, and that faith attacked Catholicism, which still was the backbone of England. Today under the late King, there might be no hangings, no gallows on the English hillsides, never long vacant, but a form of peace which the King had ordered. If Mary was proclaimed, then there would be all those renewed burnings at Tyburn, the deaths, and torture in this, The Tower. But apparently the people would rather accept this, than the quiet charming girl, whom the old 'Ragged Bear' had presented to them, as being their Queen.

'Queen Mary,' they screamed. 'Not Queen Jane. Queen Mary is the daughter of a King and

Queen, and she *is* the right person.'

The battle was being won on the cause of faith, not because of either woman. Resistance was everywhere, and the agony was, *what* would happen next?

★ ★ ★

Measures were taken in private circles to fight for the rightful queen, measures about which the girl Jane knew nothing, for it was kept from her. Northumberland had decided to depute Suffolk to command the forces, which were hurriedly being drawn together. They were massed to 'fight for the Queen', and to this they added that 'this was the Queen, whom the late King Edward—God rest his soul in peace—had desired should follow him.'

Northumberland had plans; he wanted if possible to gain possession of Princess Mary and bring her in close custody to London, but somehow the girl Jane got news of this, for people talked. She begged them to show mercy at all costs, for this *was* the daughter of a King and a Queen, and this was not what the late King would have wished. She insisted they must use mercy, little realizing how little they would give to her, when her hour came.

Northumberland wished to stay at headquarters, and organize everything, for he had been responsible for the entire affair and was determined that only the one brain could see it through properly. He was a far more experienced soldier than was Suffolk, but he felt when it came to the attack, his place was here in the city, and here in the city he *would stay*.

At Durham House he mustered a Council and never for a moment did he betrray any sign of misgivings. Privately he must have realized that things were going badly, and that he was fighting an indomitable foe in Mary, for she would stop at nothing!

He dined well (wine was ever a help), then interviewed Jane again in her room, at The Tower. Neither of them realized then the speed at which the world was turning, for they would never meet again. Over the whole world there hung the distressing shadow of treachery. None knew who was for which queen, nor even which was the *right* queen. Nor how! Nor why!

'Do not leave me too long, my uncle,' Jane begged him, for she, poor girl, was aware of pressure in the air, and afraid of what could happen next.

'Have no fear, my sweet girl! I go to bring the crown personally to your brow. I shall walk behind you to the throne in the Abbey,' and then he kissed hands.

He kissed hands with a smile, and looking up saw tears in her eyes. 'War is no part of me,' she said sorrowfully, 'and I do not wish the death of any single man, neither enemy nor friend. But this is already happening. Fear surrounds me, and I beg that we press on but without wounding and men dying. Let us go ahead, with the soul of the Protestant Church with us. I pray for it, and for all of us, too.'

It was no use arguing, she should have known it.

Next morning there departed from the capital, those men who were prepared to 'fight the Queen's enemies'. Six hundred fighting men going to the east coast, where the trouble lay. They marched through the streets with never a cheer. It was stated at that time, by Northumberland himself, to his second-in-command, 'The people come out to see us go by, but not a man of them wishes us God speed.'

TEN

> Faint friends when they fall out, most cruel foemen bee.
>
> *Edward Spenser*

POOR Jane felt wretchedly alone in The Tower even if her husband was lodging in the same place, yet he did not approach her. In her secret mind she must have known how badly things were going, and how wrong it was that the dreadful cloud of doubt should hang over the entire community.

Those in charge tried to hide their anxiety. Each man began to think more of himself and the best way to escape from an awkward set of circumstances, without letting the girl see this. They had believed that as the late King had willed it, she must climb on to his throne to follow him, now they were not so sure that this was the law.

Doubt prodded them, and left scars.

On July the 16th, a Sunday, Ridley preached at St. Paul's to a mass of people, and he pleaded Jane's cause, begging those who had "good minds and proper" to follow her, and help her ascend the throne as had been the desire of the late king. He spoke of Mary, and those who had died for her, of the tortures, the rack, the burnings and the horrors with which she was so well acquainted. It is doubtful if he impressed many, for England was in a state of cold horror! They knew too well what it was to live with the shrieks of those burning to death in their ears, and the constant tortures and beheadings at The Tower. Then one lost loved relatives, who had done no harm; torture, and death were everyday.

One prays that much of this was kept from the poor young Queen in The Tower, though surely some of her servants brought back news?

On July the 19th the horror came.

Arundel was the first man who had come

forward boldly, declaring himself to be on the side of the rightful Queen Mary. He did this, so he said, urged by conscience and anxiety for peace for the people. Pembroke backed him. Suddenly it seemed, for no reason as far as one could see, that in this hour, those who in a few days had praised the troops which had marched away to fight. But it seemed that in these hours the more noble qualities were dead. The battle progressed and Catholicism had the accessories which the Protestants had not.

The end was sudden. Men came to the Palace of The Tower to take possession. The horrifying thing for them all was that the moment he knew that he was beaten, Suffolk added his wretched signature to the proclamation to Mary as being "the just Queen of this land". Matters moved fast. The declaration was read in Cheapside to an enthusiastic scene. Had these people forgotten the vehemence of Mary, how savage she was, and how greedy ever for vengeance?

When poor Jane had been proclaimed Queen, the announcement had met with a sullen silence. But *nine* days earlier, and in those nine days everything had changed and the crowd shrieked for Queen Mary.

Bonfires were lit, their glow came in a sickeningly gory light and reflected on the grim walls of The Tower itself. The girl could see them. Joy bells rang—she heard them—and she must have known then there could be but the one end, the dreadful end of despair.

It happened that very day that certain private arrangements had been made for the baptism of a certain little child, born to Underhill (a gentleman prisoner in The Tower). Jane had promised to act as godmother to the babe, and had said that her husband, Guildford, would give his name to it also.

'Whatever happens to England now, I can scarce go back on my word to be godmother to the child,' Queen Jane said.

The Princess Mary was a remorseless woman who did not care who died, for her main grievance in living life, was with those who *lived*. If she came to the throne, and at this (the very last hour) it looked as if there was only the remotest chance of her failing, then there would be reprisals, and they would be bitter.

For some two or three days now, poor Jane had realized that everything was going wrong, and how she longed to return to the Dower Palace, whose quiet gardens were lapped by the Thames, or to the palaces where she had been so happy with Queen Katherine, poor lady!

There was still a further speech which she was told that she had to make to the Lords of the Council. If the words that she spoke were self-chosen, one is inclined to doubt it, for they do not sound the sort of thing that a girl of her tender age *would* have said! She stood before them gallantly, and not afraid. She was extremely fearless in some ways and this served her in good stead.

She said, 'Which of you can boast with truth, that I besought him to make a Queen? Where are the gifts I promised, or gave on this account? Did ye not drag me from my literary studies, where I was so happy, and, depriving me of my liberty, place me in this rank? Alas! How well I see (but far too late), to what end ye send me in this royal dignity. How well you escape the infamy following upon such foolish deeds?' and then, 'but be of good cheer, with the same measure it shall be meted to you again.'

Then she left them, under guard.

She found now that all the glory was gone, and the sweet smell of clean straw and of flowers, for she was put into a small cell, and those of her servants who had the opportunity to avail themselves of the chance, now deserted her. She turned to a strange lady.

'But why am I brought here? I am no common prisoner, as all the world knows?'

'It is the rule, Madam.'

'It is a *prison* cell.'

The woman bowed. 'That is true, Madam, and you are a prisoner of the Queen's right.'

She said, a little bitterly, 'The Queen is my cousin, and my good friend! She would not do this to me, I vow,' but the woman said nothing.

She stayed where she was put. Those who waited on her were strangers, and when night came, the girl who had never before in her whole life undressed herself, had to take off her gown, and fine linen.

'But why cannot I have my own maid?' she asked.

'It is forbidden,' the woman told her.

'I have never sinned, nor have I ever been disloyal to the Queen's majesty, as I do swear! Why am I treated thus?'

The woman shrugged her shoulders as she picked up a pile of clothes which the poor girl had just taken from her body. Jane watched, then she said, 'I trust in God, for He who brought me into this world, will save me now, and in the hour of my death.'

Next day, when the weather was overcast, and the fog hung sourly over the Battersea marshes, she was told that she would be taken back to Syon House. She thought of how she had left this mansion, but a few days previously, and had come as Queen of England in majesty, to this great Tower, built on the water's edge, with its towers and cupolas, with its majesty on the palace side, and its cruelty on the other one, the prison side.

Now, without any dignity at all, she embarked, and was rowed down to Syon again. The fields were sopping, and a high wind had blown down the wild flowers rampant in the ditches. She had travelled before as a royal queen this way but a few days previously, and had then been unable to believe that the country was hers and that she had succeeded King Edward the Sixth, which she *had* done! Now everything was completely changed!

She had never wished to be a queen, but the fact that she had reigned for the period of ten days, and for ten days only, was a thought she would have to fight, and in the end for it, possibly she might suffer.

She knew the Queen too well to expect forgiveness of her, for though a highly pious lady for ever on her knees before her *Prie Dieu*, she was spiteful in the extreme! She did not forgive her enemies, and was not prepared to give any man in the world up for a crown. She would wed, of course, her adviser would ask sons of her, and do all that they could to see that she got them. Anything could happen, but for the people who were playing leading rôles in this quite dreadful pageantry there was no hope ahead.

Coming back to Syon, she found a woman servant whom she knew, and who was set to wait on her.

'I come back to die here,' the girl said.

'But that cannot be true. Take comfort that it is a lie,' the woman said.

'Who can save me?' and she said it in despair. 'I, who would not raise a hand to destroy a fly, will die because I could not fight to get my name cleared.'

'Nothing like that has happened!' the woman said. 'So far her Royal Highness has been quite calm. You are here in the room you love best, and are free to go where you will, and as you will. You have come home, Madam. Rejoice for this.'

She had come home and now she prayed that she could contract some malady, and die here; she said so.

She said, 'But what can lie ahead for me? The Queen would never tolerate me as a competitor, though God forbid that I should ever think of that ... I am innocent, and have acted perchance foolishly, but only because I did what I was told to do.'

'This will be remembered, Madam.'

'I wonder,' and then, in a half-whisper, 'I dream of the coldness of The Tower, and the misery of dying there with all the world to see it happen.'

'You are not dead yet, Madam, and whilst you are alive there is the eternal hope.'

It was a spurt of good weather, and she grew braver when walking in the gardens, which she had always loved, and in speaking to servants, and such. But all the time, she recalled that the new Queen was one of those women who could never forgive, for her one desire was invariably vengeance, and becoming Queen of England was hardly likely to minimise her cruelty or her determination to make all submit to her will! As to the poor new church, she thought with horror, that would curl up and die, for it could have no future. She wept then for the death of the poor young boy King, who had done so much for his country and who, had he lived, could have done so much more in a manner that was noble.

Now the poor girl was cut off from communication with other people, and was distracted. Only one of the women with her was a girl whom she knew, and who had been her maid when she was a girl. The chance to speak alone to one another seldom came, and she got little news from her. Cut off from the world she waited, and for what? Where was her husband now? She had little idea! What had happened to her father and Northumberland, who had staged the entire scene, and had been so sure that the plans were watertight, and that there could be no redress?

He had not for a moment appreciated the enormity of the tidal wave of life rising against him. Inspired by the love of faith, every Catholic in the country turned against the girl who had accepted the throne, and with vehemence, and indignation! Although Mary herself was unpopular, she had a vicious temper, could be very cruel, and difficult, and few individually would have fought for her, they were fighting for a principle, the return of their birth faith, and although they had been completely happy under the Protestant régime, they were only too eager to fight now, *for* the old régime!

One night, Jane, her maid Matilda with her, had come to bed, and it was possible to talk very softly so that none could hear.

'You have no news?' poor Jane asked her.

'None at all.'

'My husband, what has happened to him?'

'They do say that he is a prisoner, and kept in The Tower of London, and that his being there was one reason why you were dismissed to come down here.'

'My father?'

'He, also, is a prisoner.'

When she thought about it, she was convinced that neither of them would be forgiven their association with her, and both would be axed. Of herself she could not be sure. She had written to the Queen, stating fully her part in her accession, and everything that had happened. She had no desire to be the Queen, nor to accept the crown, which she felt belonged to her cousin, even if the late King—God rest his soul—had left it to her.

She had been led by the male members of her family, and under their influence had come to The Tower of London, as was necessary, if she were to be made the Queen.

Simplicity and sincerity were both part of this sad girl's character, and most truthfully, she explained how foolish she had been to obey when she did the wrong thing, confessed to her sin, and sought pardon of it. The letter naturally brought no reply.

Mary could only see the action *as* sin, sin against herself, and the whole thing rested with that. But from what she did in the first few weeks of her reign, it does not look as if she seriously blamed poor Jane for what had happened, and she did nothing to add to her discomforts or to make her more unhappy.

She did not attempt to take action against this girl, and one would have thought nothing but immediate action would satisfy her. She kept her prisoner, it is true, because there was little else that she could do, and her advisers were strongly advising her that the girl should die. Her life was a menace to the Queen's strength. Mary insisted that she could not consent that she should die! She stayed firm on this.

In her letter, she had explained that she had known nothing of the plot to make her Queen, nor would she have consented to it.

'Her life is dangerous to you, Madam,' she was told by her advisers.

'Even so, I cannot bring myself to take it.' And then she asked if they would wish her to pardon His Grace of Northumberland, who had been behind the entire plan, and who had himself stirred into action those who had risen against her, even to the putting of another girl in her place on the throne.

She was told that Northumberland now was of little real threat to her. The real threat lay in the girl whom the late King had willed to take his place, and whilst she lived, she would be a constant trouble to the new Queen.

But Mary was not easily persuaded. She was Queen and gave the orders and she had loved her cousin. She kept poor Jane where she was, but of course in the end the Wyatt Rebellion forced her hand. For the moment she took revenge on others. On August the 18th Northumberland was brought before the peers in Westminster and condemned to death. His sentence was however postponed for quite a time, they said it would take place in the new year, not yet.

The little maid, Matilda, brought poor Jane the news, and she went very white.

'Even if sentence is postponed to plead Her Majesty's own wishes, in the end he is sure to die.'

'I will search for further news, Madam,' said the girl.

'I doubt if there is any news that can be pleasant news,' and the girl sighed wretchedly! 'I fear much, I know Mary and when she is roused she knows no mercy. She will say that he fought against her.'

'We must wait.'

But Matilda did not know how to comfort

her. They walked beside the river at evening, with the first faint quivering of gold in the trees, and the willows thinning on the riverbank. They were the ones who died early.

'You think there is no hope, Matilda?'

'There can be but little hope,' said the girl, 'for he cannot deny that which he did, and good men and true, died for his deeds.'

'But pardon is noble.'

'I doubt a pardon.'

When she thought about it, the girl herself also doubted, and learnt later that night, that Northumberland was condemned and would die later. The girl was deeply distressed, no pardon would come to them that was certain and she learnt that the sentence would be carried out on August the 21st, Matilda promised to get news for her. At noon of that day she admitted it, but spoke only in a whisper, as they walked by the river.

'It was eight in the morning,' she said, 'and he came to the scaffold and addressed the people, then knelt and prayed, and spoke the Creed in Latin.'

'And then...?'

'He was beheaded when the moment came, and with him Sir Thomas Palmer, and Sir John Gates.'

'And all died?'

'All *died*,' said Matilda.

The girl twined her hands together, and

twisted them. 'Why is it that I live, and these others go? Why does she keep me alive, almost as if she knew the truth, and has pity on me, but does not free me?'

'Your freedom *will* come, Madam.'

Jane shook her head. 'Far more likely the deed for my execution signed by herself,' she said wretchedly.

But none feels that the Queen is not ready to dismiss her cousin; one would hardly think that the ties of childhood's loyalties would hold her, nor that she would be kindly treated, and in the end liberated but this was apparently wrong.

The Queen had got the taste of blood in her mouth!

Possibly she had never thought to get to the throne and the first taste of savagery and personal gain, filled her with cheer, so that she could not stay herself. Everything had happened with great good fortune, almost too good to be true. Returning to her capital city, had been a dream, which perhaps she had always dreamt in those years when she had been the outcast. During that time she had nursed a hatred of the new faith which her father had introduced and tolerated. In her only words, 'It was only to do right and to make legal his marriage with the Boleyn girl!' Now that was over. She had ridden into London with the Earl of Arundel just ahead of her, and bearing the Sword of State, which was the royal symbol of her establishment as the

Queen.

Behind her had ridden her sister Elizabeth as next in order to the throne, though whether she was ever likely to become queen at that hour was dubious. Elizabeth was very thin, with piercingly bright eyes which missed nothing, and the light red hair of her father.

In that hour both women knew that history was being made, and neither could imagine what would happen next! Elizabeth had loved her father, whom Princess Mary had hated, and with just reason. Elizabeth was most unlikely to take any reckless course of action. She would bide her time doing nothing to bring her into ill-odour, and to remain calm.

That had been Mary's moment, and in some ways it had turned her head, but she maintained that she would *not* destroy Jane. Within a few days the Queen was even speaking of setting Jane free, though it never got further than the thought. She actually sent in a priest to comfort the girl. It almost seemed that her coming to the throne of England, had changed the Princess Mary, and that she *was* recovering her status, and behaving in a new manner, which was gratefully received.

Prelates told her that she must wed! England would expect this of her, and ask her to give them a Prince of Wales. This was a new idea to a sour woman, who had believed that she had missed the lists of love. She had to admit that the idea had a certain enchantment of its own, which made her feel happier.

A list of the suggested princes was brought to her. There was the King of Denmark, a Prince of Spain, and another from Portugal, also a Prince of Piedmont. One has to remember that, in those days, all these were little countries, and the kings small; it would be possible to arrange this.

Mary was a rich woman! England was rising out of the mire, and coming up again, and she could be looked upon as being something of a "catch", though perhaps less prepossessing for the man who had the misfortune to "catch her".

She now pictured herself enjoying those pleasantries which had been outside her ken. She would have a son to hold the crown secure for her, and that thought was intriguing.

Her coronation would be illustrious, with her sister, the Princess Elizabeth, carrying the crown behind her. On the face of things the old quarrels had gone, and the sisters were friends! Mary was destined to be a lonely woman all her life, because she was that sort of nature, and her quick ability to take offence tormented others, and maddened them. She was ever ready to fly into a temper.

England debated on the question as to whom the new Queen would espouse? And when? Also, what could be done with the Lady Jane Grey, and her husband?

In prison, in the house she knew so well, Jane did little, because there was nothing that she *could* do! She had given up all hope of regaining her freedom. If it was going to happen, it would have been by now, she told herself, at the beginning, not at the end of the Queen's reign.

She heard that she would be brought to trial.

Matilda had heard the news. It was whispered in city brothels. Said it would decry the others, and proclaim Mary as the good and rightful Queen, whilst Jane had been nothing but an interloper. Cranmer was to go to trial, he of all men. It was a topsy turvy world.

At this time Jane was just seventeen, and a girl who was not "old for her years". 'This is a dreadful ruling,' she said aghast.

'But the news is true, Madam,' Matilda assured her, 'and in London, all talk of it.'

'They would try me I suppose?'

'That is discussed, Madam.'

'But how can they try me when I have committed no sin?' she asked aghast.

'Queens can do strange things. My Lord Cranmer is also to be tried.'

'But what has he done?'

'He was a Protestant.'

She said, 'The Princess Elizabeth is a confessed Protestant yet she is not being brought to trial.'

'I know, but she is the Queen's sister.'

'That would make no difference, and should

make no difference,' Matilda went on. 'Her turn will come. She may think that she will never know the inside of The Tower of London, but the day *will* come for her, as well as for others.'

Jane sighed. She *had* known the inside of The Tower of London, in both its disguises, as palace, with fresh clean sweet-smelling straw, with fine curtains, hangings, and flowers, and the other side, (the prison side) where people did not bother themselves.

'I pray that her day will not come,' said Jane gently. 'She was always a kind girl, and we loved her. Her poor mother suffered so much. She indeed, knew The Tower of London, and it ended her life.'

She thought for a moment that maybe there had come the hour when the new Queen was mending her ways! Could she be changing? She had herself experienced the most terrible of lives, and this should in some ways excuse her for her malice. Could it be that, as her brother had done with success, she was trying to go back on hardship in the name of justice, and make life easier for the people? Edward had hated burnings, and the sacrifices of living people; he would have done away with cruelties of this kind. Yet Mary had condemned the Duke of Northumberland to die, though what other sentence she could have passed on him, none knew. Mary was the sovereign, and she had been brought here to accept her rights, when already they had been handed on to another. And she *had* done nothing more, save continued imprisonment against that other, her cousin the little Lady Jane, now just seventeen years of age.

Northumberland had died, yet how she could have kept him alive, was difficult to imagine! The girl in captivity and living here ever speculative of tomorrow, and worrying herself about it, realized and accepted this.

'So far Queen Mary has done nothing against you,' the girl Matilda told her, 'I am sure that she would mend her ways, and call a halt, for you have never really sinned.'

'Save that I *was* Queen,' and then, tearfully, 'I never desired this. I was happy with my studies, and would have stayed content with them. Yet none seem to realize this. Those made me a Queen, and I would have chosen to be a commoner.'

The summer died slowly.

It had been glorious weather, the flowers lasting far longer than usual, the world sweet with the scent of them, as though it was a festival, and a season which was loth to die. Autumn came late, and had caught a reflection of that beautiful summer when it came.

The coronation (often postponed) was arranged with undue haste to take place in early October, and meanwhile all manner of bargaining was proceeding on the subject of the

Queen's marriage. Her sister Elizabeth encouraged her to wed, and gave her the feeling of exhilaration and of desire for an heir. They were (outwardly) on excellent terms, but the younger of them was being careful.

It was a worry that there were people in the world who showed affection for Elizabeth, called for her, when she appeared in public, and made themselves noticeable in her cause. It made Elizabeth extremely nervous. She knew her sister better than to trust her.

Then came also the elder sister's insistence about her faith and Elizabeth recognized the danger of this. She was as Protestant as her brother had been, and it could be dangerous to refuse the older faith. Mary looked old; she was much lined and at times, sour. Elizabeth had the gaiety and the goodwill of a girl who is in love with life, but she knew that she *had* to do what the Queen said.

She attended Mass and asked that lesson books be supplied her so that she could go into the matter of the Faith, which had been considerably altered before it was restored. In the September she actually accompanied the Queen to Mass, and started arrangements for a private chapel to be put into her own house.

To turn back to the Catholic faith, could save a man's life, and it was happening everywhere, and undoubtedly it did make her own life much more secure.

The coronation came.

Elizabeth followed her sister as next to wear the crown, and carried it herself. On that very day there is a disastrous note in the history of England. Cranmer had crowned kings, and was now in imprisonment, destined to die. He was a prisoner in The Tower and in the very cell where the Duke of Northumberland had been before his death. There was, of course, no chance of mercy for him. This was *not* the age of mercy!

For the moment England was occupied on the matter of the Queen's marriage, and when Parliament met again, on October the fifth, it seemed that somewhere or other the partnership had been finally settled. There had been many noble princes who had offered themselves, but the one which the Queen herself most favoured, was the one from her mother's country. Undoubtedly, she felt the pull this way, because of her mother coming from Spain, for he was not an attractive man. There seemed little doubt that he was the man selected, and soon there would be a royal wedding, and later the birth of a Prince of Wales. For, although Mary looked very old for her years, her face fallen away, and her eyes tired, and lined, she was still young enough to have a child.

Just at the hour of coronation another move was made.

There came back to The Tower of London,

Lady Jane and her husband, travelling quietly by barge from her home to The Tower itself. Perhaps she had guessed that this must come—she was privately sure of it.

'We go to death,' she told Matilda.

'That is not certain, Madam. Remember that some have been released when they got there. Though they were bound for prison and further sentence, they found that freedom was their gift into the future.'

'That will not be for me,' she said slowly.

'You cannot tell. There are rumours that a pardon will be issued for you. I did hear the city discussing it only the other day.'

'She would not trust me again,' and the voice was infinitely sad. It might have been the tone of a woman nearing forty, rather than of a girl who was just seventeen years of age.

She hated the feeling that for ever the sword hung over her. She dreaded the remembrance of months spent in prison, and she unable to state her case or say a word in her own favour.

'I think it is coming to an end,' said Matilda kindly, 'and on her wedding day she will free you, as a special favour.'

It was possible. It was the sort of coincidental gift that Queen Mary *had* made at different times. The cell into which she was put was not unpleasant, she had to admit this, and some trouble had been made to make it more attractive for her. That, of course, was a good sign she should have felt but was too sick at heart and too sad to feel anything like this.

She asked if there were any news of a trial and was told that nothing had been arranged, which she believed, though even at that very hour the plans were going ahead.

The coronation was the great subject of the day, with all London singing far into the night, rolling in the streets, and fighting when they got too drunk! The girl lay awake in her prison cell listening to it and at moments weeping about it. The noise was very clear, the people were happy! Had they already forgotten that she lay here, and soon could die? She told herself no plans for her trial were made as yet. There was no talk of them, and that should comfort her.

'Take heart,' said Matilda, 'bad news travels fast, you would know.'

Within a few hours of the last merriment and adventures celebrating the coronation, it happened. The city was quietening down again, and becoming more itself, when the news was brought for her.

She had awakened that day with the feeling of something terrible to hand, and when the Governor came to tell her, knew instantly that it would take all the courage that she could bring into her life, to take this calmly, and, as a queen!

The trial had been finally arranged to be held at Guildhall, on the thirteenth of November. That same day the trials of others would be conducted there, my Lord Cranmer, with Guildford the girl's husband, his brother, and herself. They would travel there by foot.

She said, 'I pray God that I can bear it.'

'They may free you,' said the Governor, though he knew this was impossible. She would have been quietly freed before had the Queen ordained it, a silent sort of arrangement, with little comment, and she would have slipped away into the unknown. But something had happened which had made Mary decide against this method and this was what she had done.

'Pray God I have the strength to accept it,' she said.

'God will be with you.'

'I pray so,' she whispered.

★ ★ ★

She never knew how she lived through that dreadful period of waiting, and knowing that every hour brought the final scene nearer, and behind that the figure of the masked headsman, with the axe in his hand. For they *would* kill her! Of this she was convinced, as with the passing weeks the depression became more deadly. Her husband could do nothing, of course; like herself, he was a prisoner, and an entirely guiltless one. Jane knew Mary well enough to realize how harsh she was!

'I should have died before this,' she told

Matilda.

'Maybe you lived because God willed it, and as she has waited so long, the Queen will spare you.'

She shook her head. She remembered the arbitrary way of the Queen, and how when they were young and she played games with them, she always waited for just the right moment to play her trump card. 'She spares no one,' she said softly.

'But her own cousin...?'

'That only enhances the need to destroy me. I could be the heir to something that she has, and now will keep. She will reign and England will weep that they ever set her on the throne. Mary can be cruel, deeply cruel.' And then, with tears in her eyes, 'I shall not live to see Christmas again, I know it.'

She thought sadly of those Christmases spent at Hampton Court Palace, when Henry was the King, and how he had played with the children, and had laughed with them. If he were back, even for a few hours, everything would be changed again. It would be Mary who would go to the block, she was sure of that.

She said, sadly, 'Not one in every fifty brought to trial, escapes the fatal sentence,' and she said it coldly, 'both my husband and I will die. God decreed it! I did wrong in letting them bring me to the throne, and doing what Edward wished, and willed me to do. I knew at the time it would not help me. I did wrongly, and I shall pay for this?

* * *

The day of the trial was dreary. A fog hung over the river for weeks, it seemed, and smudged out the Battersea marshes across it and on the far banks. The smell which Jane disliked most seemed to penetrate everywhere and they went on foot to the Guildhall. Cranmer was there; he was composed and calm but quite sure of the sentence, did his best to comfort the others. Jane, her husband, and his brother, the men all coming first.

There had been no big crowds to meet them, the girl had half expected that many would have assembled, seeking perhaps to help her, but she knew already that it was far too late for help. "We all are doomed and have heard our sentences before we go to the court", she thought, and tried to compose herself. She was ill! She had been suffering from a very bad cold, for The Tower was hideously damp, the walls ran with water at times. She had difficult fits of coughing, only praying this would not make the trial longer, for, when the attacks came, they lasted quite a while.

She wore a black dress feeling that it represented mourning for herself, and within her, there was no hope. When her time came, she pleaded guilty, which surprised all there. In a firm voice she said that, under the guidance of others, and believing that she did the right thing, as her masters instructed her, she had behaved wrongly. It was exactly what had happened; she had never had any such wish to be queen and she said so. If it came to guilt, she blamed herself.

It was doubtful if she ever heard the sentence of death which was pronounced upon her. It could be by the axe or by fire, as she knew, and shuddered at the thought of fire! It is doubtful if she ever even heard the words as they were read out, for no change came into her eyes or face, and as she turned away, she broke down in a violent fit of coughing.

Guildford tried to help her, himself condemned, as was the Archbishop; he looked to be unbelievably young as she did, one could not believe that either of them were more than children, but they had received a grown man's sentence, and without a doubt, it *would* be carried out!

On their way back to The Tower there was a crowd. They had heard what was happening, and came out of their houses. There was the first feeling of rage against the Queen, about whose reign a witch had predicted that "the streets would flow with blood, and the screams from Tyburn would be heard echoing as far as Oxford itself".

Now they learnt that the condemned were coming forth from the Guildhall and would walk back to The Tower in close custody. Men surged out of the inns and the brothels, women with them. The girls from the brothels marked Guildford's good looks, and the cool deportment of his brother, as if neither of them cared what had happened. The Archbishop was completely composed, he might be returning home to a comfortable meal, and he lifted his hand in blessing on the waiting crowd.

They stared, and shrieked pity, and harped on the gross injustice, particularly with the young girl, pale as death itself, but walking calmly. The boy and girl were tragically young to die, but as the crowd must have known, no rising could help them! There was nothing they could do, save shriek a curse on Queen Mary and a blessing on those who died. Jane it seemed, was not so horrified about her own fault, she had, from the first, insisted that she could expect nothing else, she had obeyed her father, and her uncle, and in allowing them to bring her to The Tower as Queen, had sinned truly indeed.

But, as she said, her husband had been condemned for something which was not his fault; he had done no harm! It was cruel that he should lose a brave young life, for no sin at all.

The crowd agreed with her.

If Mary was concerned, she did not show it.

Now she was entranced with plans for her coming marriage. As Queen she could not stay a maid, for the country required an heir. They had had trouble enough with looking for an heir to the throne, when King Edward the Sixth had died, and this had been where all his anxiety had begun.

She had decided to marry the Prince of Spain. It is impossible to say that her mother's alliance decided Queen Mary. The time had come when action was necessary, the waiting time when she had had doubts had come and gone; she took action.

Jane was retired to The Tower a prisoner, bewildered and down at heart, others with her. The journey was made at night, lest there should be any signs of opposition, poor Jane supposed, and she never spoke a word as the grim doors of The Tower closed behind her. She knew it was the end.

Her quarters had been changed, and she had been given the small cell where poor young Kathryn Howard had slept, when she was awaiting the end, and with such tremendous courage! The thought of that dark-eyed Kathryn whom it was admitted, had sinned, but it had been the sin of youth. She had had gaiety, and in the long run must have found her husband's age tedious when she was so alive with youth.

It was here that brave Kathryn had asked to

see the block, could it be brought to her? She had ever feared strange things, but she would not fear the day she died, she said.

They had brought the block to her.

Entering the cell Jane hesitated, and went very white, for she knew who had occupied it before her, and also knew it meant the end.

'If I could have some water?' she begged. 'I feel faint....'

The Governor was a kind man, and, although the girl had four official matrons with her night and day, he told Matilda to bring fresh water to her.

'They will not take Matilda from me?' Jane asked him.

'No, Madam, I give you my word. She will stay.'

'Till the end? Promise me that?' she implored.

'Yes, Madam, until the end.'

He remarked later to his wife that the poor young girl looked considerably older than a year ago, when she had first met him. Now the long imprisonment had seemed to be endless, and for every prisoner facing the death sentence, the prayer for a reprieve is the flag of truce, which they fly. But she had no hope. Her very presence was too dangerous to permit her to live. She would have to die.

Later, she asked the kind Governor, if he had news of her husband, for she knew little of him, and none would tell her.

'My husband?' she asked.

'Yes, Madam.'

'I am sick for him, and none of this was his fault that this happened. He has no royal blood in his veins, and no right to the throne of England! The late King—God rest his soul—left me the throne, and if my husband is to die, merely because he wedded me, what is his crime? Is he to suffer?'

The Governor tried to parry the moment. 'He is still *your* husband,' he reminded her.

'But he is *not* a Tudor.'

'No, but a relation of them.'

'It is unfair.' She could get no news because Matilda and those dire matrons, were here; she was never permitted to be alone and a woman janitor was for ever in her cell. She did not sleep alone, she was for ever conscious of that other presence, and disliked it intensely.

At the palace the Queen hardly noticed what was happening, so thrilled was she with the thought of acquiring a husband, a consort who would give her a boy prince to follow her to the throne. If she had had happy dreams, and she had done this, there had never been any romantic ones. She knew that she was plain. She had never thought to be in the arms of a man, but now she saw ahead of her, the joy of marriage and a honeymoon, later herself bearing a young prince.

If she thought of Jane at all (which is dubious) it would have been with some agony of spirit, and with regrets. But she so loathed the Church of England that she would have done anything to tear it down, and Jane had been entirely Protestant. By nature, Mary was unsympathetic; most of the Tudors were born hard-hearted.

It is fantastic that during this time, and it was a considerable time, none had buried the boy King, who still lay almost a skeleton not interred. This must have struck the Queen. Suddenly she allowed him to be buried, and she made what was an enormous sacrifice for her, he was buried according to the ritual of the reformed Prayer Book. She had a Requiem Mass sung for him in The Tower, with hundreds present, and many to mourn him. Since this woman had come to the throne, there had been too much happening!

Some said that perhaps Queen Mary had lost her perverse severity of outlook, her harshness, and would develop a remarkable leniency and practise a tenderness to which hitherto she had been averse. Jane had returned to The Tower and to the death cell, her husband also, she believed, and there was no possibility of escape.

In The Tower one heard strange sounds, those to which the walls did never become accustomed. The eternal drip of water, the tide beating against the walls; the shrieks of those undergoing torture, and the worse horror, of the giggling chattering crowd, coming to view the latest beheading, almost as if they laughed their way into some gay entertainment and enjoyed it.

Pray God, do not let this last long! she prayed.

ELEVEN

To be, or not to be; that is the question;
Whether 'tis nobler in the mind to suffer
The slings and arrows of outrageous fortune,
Or to take arms against a sea of troubles,
And by opposing end them? To die—to sleep—
No more; and by a sleep to say we end
The heart-ache, and the thousand natural shocks
That flesh is heir to—'tis a consummation
Devoutly to be wished.
William Shakespeare

IN prison poor little Lady Jane Grey wrote one letter, and also put an inscription added to the Lieutenant of The Tower Bridge to put in the same book. This book has this inscription, addressed to him, apparently at his request.

Foreasmuch as you have desired so simple a woman as myself to write in so worthy a book,

good Master Lieutenant, therefore I shall as a friend desire you and, as a Christian require you, to call upon God to incline your heart to His laws and quicken you in His way, and not to take the word of truth utterly out of your mouth. Live still to die, that by death you may purchase eternal life, and remember the end of Methuselah, who, as we read in the Scripture, was the longest liver that was of a man, died at the last; for as the preacher saith, there is a time to be born, and a time to die, and the day of death is better than the day of our birth.
    Yours, as the Lord Knoweth as a friend,
Jane Dudley.

Now as she lay here under sentence itself, her amiable walks which she had been permitted in the gardens of The Tower were ended. Nor could she visit the Queen's garden any more.

There was a story going the rounds, that Guildford (also waiting to die within these cruel walls) desired an interview with his wife, and he said that he desired to give her the last kisses and embraces. But she was the one who refused this request, possibly because she felt that she could not muster the courage to face it. They had parted when sentenced, surely that was the better end? The story went, that Queen Mary would not permit them to see each other, but it was Jane herself, who stood in the way.

Neither of them knew when the hour would

be, nor where, though it looked as though it might be on Tower Hill where so many others had died. Now the young girl thought of poor Anne Boleyn who gone with such brave calm to the block, and had been magnificent to the crowd who returned feeling deep sympathy with so courageous a woman.

There had been the Howard girl who had actually, on the scaffold, declared her love for Tom Culpepper, and had stated that she would rather have died his wife, than wife of the King!

Jane behaved differently.

She had none of Anne's pride, nor had she Kathryn' strong prevalent courage. She loved lesson books and learning, not men, and she came quietly, almost like a nun.

It had previously been planned that she and Guildford would die together, and then Matilda found this was changed. It was feared lest the crowd became difficult, and the next plan was for Guildford to die on Tower Hill, whilst Jane died, as originally arranged, where Anne Boleyn and Kathryn Howard had died, within the precincts of The Tower itself.

'This is true?' the girl asked.

Matilda said, 'An old servant told me, and it was correct.'

'Will a huge crowd be there?'

'There will be people there, of course.'

'But not too many?'

'They will be kept from you.'

'And Dudley? I fear for him! Will they be close to Dudley?'

'I do not know, Madam. I could not discover. He—he is to die first.'

She smiled. 'We meet in Paradise,' she whispered.

'They do say that the Queen is afraid of public opinion.'

'I can believe that.'

'Take heart, Madam. Life does curious things, even now!'

She shook her head.

Queen Mary played her cards slowly, but she played them to assure her own safety and Jane could rest assured of this. How could a Queen hope to live, and reign over a country where another declared Queen dwelt? She could not have included Queen Anne of Cleves in this, a harmless old woman who ate plentifully, smiled with all, and had found life a pleasant dream which lasted a long time. She knew that her cousin, Queen Mary, had been badly shaken by the Wyatt rebellion, it was this which must have signed her own death sentence, Jane told herself.

She could not have gone on living in a country where her successor reigned. It would split the world into two parts, and in the end it could only bring wars, sad civil wars, and more of them.

'Find out everything that you can, I pray

you,' she begged Matilda.

'It is not easy, Madam.'

'Nothing urgent is ever easy,' said the girl slowly, and already she could feel the chill of the shadow of death upon her.

The dreadful apprehension was for ever with her. Could she dare hope for help? For rescue? Not truly so. The dreadful despair drenched her so that she felt that she almost walked in another world, for quietly everything was disappearing. Death was at hand but Matilda stayed to that sickening and bitter end.

In truth, she had never been Dudley's wife, and she had returned home from her marriage ceremony. Both of them were mere children, and the whole thought of the marriage would be ridiculous.

Hers had become a ceremony. Nothing more!

They had parted that night when the child still wore her bridal veil and she had gone back to her virgin bed with her mother. Yet now in the gloomy Tower of London both lay awaiting sentence of death. She felt that in this hour she loved the man more than she had ever done before, but she refused to let him visit her.

'It would be too sad! I committed him to this,' she said, 'I cannot make him suffer one teardrop more than the law demands of both of us. I will *not* see him again!'

'Time still could save both of you,' Matilda whispered.

'I wonder?'

'God is very good.'

'I know,' and she crossed herself piously.

'Think of *Him*,' whispered Matilda, 'He will save you all.'

★   ★   ★

Mary had been continually prompted to set the wheels of revenge in motion. She had liked her cousin and possibly left alone would not have done this, for they had played together as children and she had no bone to pick with her, save that she had deliberately permitted herself to be walked into the tragedy which now surrounded her.

It is certain that Mary cared for her cousin, that the whole thing worried her, but what could she do? Jane was a dangerous proposition to her. She had done no wrong, only acting on the instructions of others, spurred on by that wretched Northumberland and her father; she had done what she was told.

The Queen said to her ministers, 'I love my cousin, and would spare her if I could, but can I? Whilst she lives, she is the leader of the following which was urged on by the late King. She could take my own crown from me.'

They comforted her.

Yes, yes of course, even if she were the most forgiving woman in all the world, the girl Jane was far too dangerous to keep alive! She was the figure of the damsel in distress which always inspires a following. Young, pretty and serene, as Jane was, but, above all, a faithful Protestant. Nobody knew better than the venomous Queen Mary herself, how desperately wrong it would be to keep Jane living, even in the utmost seclusion! She would always be the figurehead to the barge of State, which could start a Protestant rising.

She had been tried and condemned, which was the only result that one could have expected, and privately Queen Mary must have sighed with some relief! It became known that the people had shown signs of vehemence, and this was what Mary dreaded. She wanted no pity for the prisoner, and would not agree to reducing the sentence. Crowds came round The Tower calling her name. Luckily, she heard nothing, for those who guarded her took good care of it. At the same time what the people did not see, was that it would have been madness to have kept Jane alive.

The original plan had been for the young husband and wife to die together, and this Queen Mary instantly turned aside. She was taking a risk with her throne, and the people were not all madly in love with her, she knew! If boy and girl died together, they would incite the admiration of romanticists, and there could easily be a rising.

The whole thing must be quieter than that, she ordered. Discretion, the royal girl was to be destroyed in The Tower, her husband outside. It would be discreet to arrange the ropes, so that the crowd were a fair distance from the prisoners. This made it less easy for a rising. She gave instructions to guard against any display of sympathetic understanding, for, deep down in her heart, she liked none of this.

Queen Mary had aged considerably in the few weeks since she had come to the throne. She resented the fact that her siser, Elizabeth, was still young, gay and striking-looking. Mary was jealous of her, far more jealous that she had ever been of Jane Grey. Elizabeth had bright-red hair like her father's had been, and she had amazing blue eyes which could blaze like savage fires when she was angry, something else that she had inherited from her outrageous father. But she had the most beautiful hands. Anne Boleyn had been born with double joints at the top of her thumbs, and detested this. It was said that when she found she was enceinte, she would pray every day that her son or daughter might not inherit this deformity, but would have beautiful hands. The child, Elizabeth, had extremely beautiful hands, as anyone could see, from her pictures.

There were two vital subjects of controversy everywhere. One was the executions of Lady Jane, and of her husband, and surely these would take place before Christmas. There was no point in waiting! In fact, Queen Mary's one agony was that something might happen! The other was her own marriage and this she looked forward to. The groom was a Spanish Prince, possibly chosen because of her mother's Spanish connections.

The Spanish Prince was not very attractive, but she chose him from a curious list of others. Whether the gentlemen themselves had any choice in the matter, lies with the gods. He was dark, his hair receding on the temples, and with a short, squat neck, which gave him the idea of being stout. This was the man whom eventually she would marry. He spoke little English, though having always chatted in Spanish with her mother, this offered no problem.

It was possible the thought of the marriage which brought Jane to trial, later took her to the block. Mary wished to get everything settled before her new life began. It is as my people desire of me, was the way that she thought of it, and smiling over it, and with time she had actually made herself believe this.

At one time she had thought that Jane could live, then it was brought to her consideration that whilst the Protestant leader lived, there could be no safety for the country. The old split between Protestants and Catholics would remain here, and none could live at peace under it.

Lying in The Tower under sentence of death, was a dreadful ordeal as Jane well knew, though they were good to her, and she was allowed what was known as 'the liberty of the Tower' which meant that she could walk at certain times of the day in the 'Queen's Garden' and on the hill. Both Guildford and his brother, lying under sentence of death as well, were given the liberty of the leads in the Bell Tower which meant that they had ample freedom and no undue restriction.

Rumour said that there was a certain amount of discontent about the Queen's coming marriage to the Spanish Prince. Although the country had loved Katherine of Aragon, she had brought them trouble in the long run and none had regretted bidding *adieu* to the Spanish influence.

In January, with the Spanish marriage approaching very near indeed, and with it what should have been a time of rejoicing, things changed. Suddenly Devonshire folk started a rising, and Exeter fell into their hands. It was shockingly cold weather, and the trouble in the county itself was followed by other counties starting what were called 'insurgencies', and there was constant fighting. War could start with surprising suddenness, and London went through much apprehension, and sense of trouble, some saying that mayors and aldermen and many of the leading citizens grew more restless than they said. It would be a shocking thing if civil war began. In this small island when trouble began, it started too fast. Now at this moment, we were nearer civil war than we had been for a long time and had it actually happened, Queen Jane might easily have been released and restored to command, whilst Queen Mary was the one who was beheaded.

But this did not happen.

The Queen's advisers warned her that she was being blind about her little cousin, and that it was unwise. Whilst Lady Jane Grey lived, there were two schools of thought in England. One believed that the Crown, and the Protestant Church should be maintained, and the other was strongly and vehemently desiring to support the Catholic Queen.

Although she had come to the throne recently it was surprising how popular Mary was, far more so than Queen Jane, but this had not endured. A change came.

Mary hated what she was doing, but she agreed with what her advisers said. She despatched her personal chaplain to see Jane, a devout Benedictine, who had once suffered imprisonment for his faith and was kind. He had no success. This brought the end nearer; it had to be. Now February the ninth was finally settled as being the day of execution for both of them, husband and wife, but *not* together.

Possibly she was at last glad that the hour had

come. It had taken too long. Anyway she would be at rest, she told herself, but a trifle sadly.

Already it was too late. Her husband sent her a little note asking leave to see her, to make their farewells. She thought about it and then refused him, feeling that it was too much to ask of either of them. There was nothing more to say!

Jane was undoubtedly a scholar, and a very religious girl. She wrote to her sister, Katherine, and told her 'Live still to die' as she had told the Lieutenant of The Tower.

On the night before the day when she was destined to die, two Bishops, and other gentlemen, talked with her for a very long time in the last hope of converting her, but in the end, they left her for she was quite determined.

Dudley wrote to her too, again trying to have a meeting with her, but she felt, possibly with truth, that this could only add to her miseries, and said that they were to meet for ever in another world so soon, and bade him *adieu*.

She was calm, almost to the extreme. Matilda was much more distracted than the girl herself, who must have been worn out with the mental suffering of the months here, and who now possibly looked upon the morrow as giving her her freedom.

'Where do I die? Here in The Tower?' she asked Matilda.

'That is the plan,' said the girl.

'He first?'

'They tell me so.'

She must have been wakened by the noise of the crowd which were collecting, both for herself and others outside The Tower on the hill.

'I wish I could have seen him once again,' she had said sadly.

That wish was answered, because on his way to the Green, Dudley was led past her window, and they saw each other. Jane spent the moments praying.

One horror was that the cart bringing the poor young man's now headless body back to his prison, came past her as she emerged to go to her own death. She knew instantly what it was, of course, and appeared to be very startled, weeping for some moments, and then she spoke.

'Guildford, oh Guildford,' she said, 'the past that you have tasted, and I soon shall taste, is not so bitter as to make my flesh tremble; for all this is nothing, to the feast that you and I shall partake this day in Paradise.'

The little speech was typical of the girl into which she had developed, the girl which she became! All her life she would have put book learning and religious faith before her romantic life, and now, at the end, this showed.

She came with Matilda her maid, and two gentlewomen, a girl grown much older in her heavy black dress, her eyes wet with tears for her lost husband, and it was said that she prayed all the way to the scaffold itself.

It was a brilliantly clear February day, with the leafless trees like black lace against the pale blue sky. She was told that she could say a few words to the populace, but that she must be quick.

She told them that her sentence was lawful, but said that she had never desired to be their Queen nor reign from the throne, that she had been given time to mourn, and to repent, and she prayed that they would assist her with their prayers.

Quietly, she knelt down, and died, a woman who had, one would say, never sinned! She was completely calm, but the crowd wept bitterly for her.

As they turned away, satisfied to have seen the gruesome sight, one old man said (and it could have been to his doom) 'Pray God that we who let her die, did the right, not the wrong thing! Pray His merciful forgiveness and beg that, in losing one sweet and gentle lady, for another who is not so gentle, we may not also lose our own heads.'

Already the tolling bell had rung for England. Ahead of them lay a few years when they would repent. Quietly at Hatfield, the Young Elizabeth wiped away her own tears, and studied carefully. She had loved her cousin well, and knew that she should have been Edward's wife. Sadly she said, 'We lost too much when the boy died. Let us pray that we have not lost everything.'

Photoset, printed and bound in Great Britain by
REDWOOD BURN LIMITED, Trowbridge, Wiltshire

```
                        C 1 lg pt ed
Bloom
The ten-day queen.


         LEE COUNTY LIBRARY
            107 HAWKINS AVE.
         SANFORD, N. C.  27330
```